JULIA'S WORLD IN TUNE

ANOTHER JULIA DEANE MURDER MYSTERY

DEBORAH M. JONES

✾ Created with Vellum

ABOUT THE AUTHOR

DEBORAH M JONES is a retired theologian with a doctorate in the ethical treatment of animals and is a Fellow of the Oxford Centre for Animal Ethics. As well as having edited a national newspaper and several journals, she has been a teacher, lecturer and music critic. Now she writes short stories, and dramas for her local radio station, for which she hosts a regular classical music show. The author lives a full life in her adopted Gloucestershire.

ACKNOWLEDGEMENTS

The Author wishes to thank all fellow members of the Burney Society for their help and encouragement, as well as all the other players of the South London Sinfonietta under the direction of Maestro Peter Fender, with whom she makes music each summer in Sicily.

The Director and Staff of the wonderful Villa Palazzola deserve thanks too for their patience and permission in allowing the Villa to be used in this work of fiction. Of course, nothing untoward would ever happen there.

PROLOGUE

Not another murder? This has got to stop. It seems that violent death follows me like the tail of a comet. Even when I leave the country — with classical musicians, of all people ...

CHAPTER 1

Late Spring

I WAS BACK ONCE AGAIN in my old North London flat. On my own, that is; without David – my husband. I was not entirely on my own as I had to share the first floor apartment with a flat-mate, Louisa, a former colleague. She had taken over the lease a year ago when, after a surge of altruism and wifely devotion, I had given up everything to follow David – soon to be promoted to Detective Chief Inspector – to the West of England. We went to care for his frail parents.

They have to manage without me, now. Too bad.

Does that sound callous? Well, let David's new girlfriend look after them.

I had mixed feelings about being back in London. This might just be a cramped and scruffy first floor apartment in an Edwardian townhouse in Camden. It could not compare with the Deanes' grand old Cotswold farmhouse, but it was a refuge. Home. Anywhere would be home, anywhere other than where he was: David. Bitter? God, yes.

I raged inside more often and more deeply than was good for me, not only at what he had done, but at the sacrifice I had been obliged to make to be with him and his parents. Especially the giving up of my university career – teaching Eighteenth Century literature, for which there is not a lot of call in the jobs market. The small field of employment was diminishing ever further with cuts to the education budget and students somehow opting for qualifications that led to high-earning careers. Unemployed academics were no great models for them.

David had stayed on with his parents; so had my mother, Helena (pronounced *Heleena*, don't ask my why). She had turned up one day at the Deanes' after I had been in a car accident, offering her help, such as it was. She so enjoyed living in the grand style in the big old comfortable house – what a surprise – that she remained after I left.

She had been a hopeless parent to me, handing me over at a young age to be brought up by her own mother, my beloved Nana Ivy. However, to my amazement Helena turned out to be a caring foster mother to Melissa, the girl from next door to the Deanes.

During the year I lived there, this poor brain-damaged teenager had been suddenly bereft of her father and just before I left had tragically lost her mother to suicide.

So, orphaned and unable to live on her own, yet terrified of new surroundings, she had gone just the short distance away to live in the Deanes' home with their blessing and that of the social services. She was still able to attend the National Star College where she enjoyed learning basic skills, and Helena mothered her in a manner I found both amazing and admirable.

When I thought of poor simple Melissa, it was with stabs of guilt at leaving her, but I had to get away. There was no alternative.

Louisa had taken the lease on my old flat jointly with her boyfriend – always a mistake, I find — but he had moved out after a quarrel. So here I was, back again, no longer mistress of the apartment, but sleeping on the sofa-divan in the sitting room and storing my clothes in what had been the ex-boyfriend's half of the wardrobe in the bedroom.

'I promise not to invade your space,' I told Louisa on moving back in. 'Just let me know when I do.'

To this she was not averse.

Quite often she would let me know. Very often, in fact. Someone you think you know from friendship in the work-place turns out quite differently in the home, it seems. I discovered the young woman I had opted to share with was nothing but a tidiness freak, an OCD sufferer (is it those who suffer, or the ones who have to live with them?), with an obsession for hygiene, tidiness to the level of minimalism, and scrupulous cleanliness. Fortunately I found a bolt-hole. The flat below mine was owned by my mother's fairly new husband, Ronald. Helena and he had met when she had landed at my door, sack of clothes in hand and demanding refuge. She had fled the Welsh commune-farm she had been living in since before I was born. One of its leaders was my biological father, a man I barely knew but with a reputation for philandering.

That sort of charismatic, exciting and irresponsible personality would be attractive to my mother, whereas I would not have believed that Ronald, retired civil servant Ronald, would have been for a moment her type: too conventional and staid. But he was smitten with her. She became fond of him and they have remained close ever since. Never prejudge people, I tell myself. But despite that, I do it all the time.

When I moved out of the Deanes' home and into the London flat, a space was created which opportunistic Helena seized upon. She invited Ronald to join her in the countryside. I doubt the Deanes were thrilled, but my mother can be very persuasive.

Dear sweet Ronald, much put-upon Ronald, rather-prone-to-loneliness Ronald, went off to Gloucestershire to join the crew that I had abandoned.

I wished the idea had been proposed before I had moved into my old flat, then I could have moved into his. I had made a solid commitment to helping Louisa with the rent, so I had to put up with it.

For the few weeks he was there below me, I enjoyed his company, calling down for the odd chat and hearing him moving around and playing his radio rather too loudly. He sensibly held on to the lease and all the furnishings, and readily agreed to the arrangement I dreamt up whereby I would keep an eye on it for him in exchange for using it at times during the day. I aired it and watered his plants, and forwarded mail that arrived for him.

I was delighted to have somewhere to go away from Louisa where I could leave papers, books and journals scattered in apparent disorder. I used her flat simply to sleep and eat in, keeping everything neat there and so reducing the opportunities for the control-freak to find fault with. I could see why her boyfriend left.

I occupied my time by completing the book on the brilliant Eighteenth Century family of the Burneys: stars of the cultural world of their time. I had a deadline to work to and an editor who kept chivvying me up to send her copy.

What I would do for a living after that was published, I had no idea. I could not return to David. Out of the question. What was the point? He did not love me, obviously. He would not have had an affair if he had. Or was still having it, for all I know. Or moved on to others. Perhaps he was just like my father had been, but had a better way of hiding his parallel lives and affairs.

Such were my frequent thoughts. Too frequent. Somehow I was holding on to my hurt, maybe even nurturing it. I felt it, thought it, perhaps even cherished it – after all, it was all I had. The rest of life, of me, was empty. A clean sheet for maybe more hurt and more betrayal. I vented my anger on social media sites, finding comfort in the Likes and Sad Faces that responded. I tried expressing my feelings to Louisa, but not for long. Her look of being hunted and desperate to escape told me to stop.

I sometimes had periods when I turned from blaming David to considering that I must be the really guilty one, that I must have forced him to find love elsewhere. Perhaps I bored him, or was too plain or dull and he found more excitement in having an affair. Maybe he had never loved me and only married me out of pity or because I or the culture, or society, had somehow pressurised him.

My emotions were draining me. From anger and guilt to numbness. I see-sawed and plateaued, like symphonic movements transitioning unequally from *allegro* to *adagio* to *presto* (fast, slow, really fast), but music with lots of discords and jarring notes. Maybe all my life would be like this. I would become a bitter old woman, incapable of feeling anything positive. Never happy again.

One day my mobile sounded, its ringtone an old-fashioned 'brrrring, brrring'.

'Hey, Julia,' sounded a welcome voice. It was Toya, a former postgraduate music student with whom I had spent some time before the Gloucestershire episode. Although I was no musician, I had helped her with her doctoral research on the musicologist and music historian Dr Charles Burney, father of the more famous Frances. It was this daughter, the 'Mother of English Literature', according to Virginia Woolf, who was my special subject of expertise. But the whole Burney family fell into my interest category. Hence the book I was finishing.

I had blogged my London friends about my return to the capital and Toya was one of my most frequent contacts. When I was feeling low, I was glad that she often communicated by telephone. The human voice can mean so much more than even the most gushing social media or email expressions. We had talked, but not yet met up. She got her question in before I could think of anything beyond 'Hey, how ya doing?'

'Are you free on Friday? I'd love you to come and meet my partner, Felix. I might have mentioned him.'

'A few hundred times!' I replied, smiling. Her conversations and social media pages were full of him.

'Oh, he's really wicked. You'll like him, I know. We are having a couple of friends round on Friday. It's Felix's birthday, plus there's someone else I need you to meet. It would be perfect. Please come.'

Intriguing.

Some near-calamitous exploits endured by Toya and me a

year or so before had drawn us close. Any friends of hers would be bound to be agreeable. I needed friends now.

I drove to the address on the appointed evening, and was impressed. Far from the drab student hostel she had occupied previously, this airy apartment was set in the semi-basement of a substantial house in Kensington. Obviously expensive, it was convenient for her college, and had street parking as a bonus. I pressed the bell and a moment later Toya opened the door to me with a beaming smile and we fell into a girl-hug on the doorstep.

'Come in, Julia. So good to see you – and you're looking great.' The Barbadian lilt in her voice seemed more pronounced than formerly. I soon found the reason for that. A tall, wildly handsome young man approached, the whiteness of his well-cut shirt contrasting starkly with his dark skin. He was as good looking as on the photographs that Toya posted.

He greeted me warmly in a bass voice with a pronounced Caribbean accent. 'Hi, I'm Felix. So good to meet you, Julia – or should I call you Doctor Deane? Toya has told me so much about you, and all you got up to. Dangerous times!'

'Hi, Felix. No, definitely not Doctor. Julia is fine, and yes, we did have some adventures, mostly best forgotten.'

I warmed to him immediately. Oh Toya, you're a lucky girl.

'Felix comes from the island, too, a fellow Barbadian,' she explained, wrapping one arm around his back. 'He works in the City, doing what – I never know!'

'Come now, let's introduce our other guests to Julia. They're all dying to meet her! A drink, Julia? Wine or rum cocktail?'

I took the proffered cocktail glass and was ushered into the living room. Several people were already there, standing chatting and sipping. A group of laughing young people was gathered around one much tattooed and pierced hipster breathily making a tune on some sort of bamboo pipe.

Two or three older people were examining an elaborately painted harpsichord in the furthest part of the room, wine glasses in hand. Felix waved over a well-dressed couple with whom he had been in coversation as I arrived.

'Julia, this is my sister, Adèle, and her husband Leon. They are both doctors at the North London Hospital. Leon is from St. Kitts, not Barbados, but we forgive him.' As I was greeting them, another, rather older man approached, having been invited to do so by Felix.

' And this is Theodore, Teddy we call him.'

'Theo sounds too much like you're calling on God,' smiled the distinguished-looking man about ten years my senior. I stood transfixed. His was the most handsome, sensitive face I had seen in years. Atop it was a thick mane of wavy, slightly greying hair. I took in his dark plum jacket with a mandarin collar which suited his trim shape. But it was his blue eyes, beaming good humour and intelligence that most captivated me.

'Teddy,' continued Felix, 'is a visiting professor at Toya's music college. A very famous conductor.'

'Well, not so very famous,' Teddy responded with a wry smile. 'In fact, hardly famous at all! I move in a rather small world, the Baroque and early classical', he enlightened me. 'And you, Julia, are just the person I've been looking for, from all that Toya has told me.'

I flushed with pleasure. Had I been on my own I would have hugged myself and danced a little jig.

To have been sought out by such a man for whatever reason was so flattering and so novel I was not sure how to handle it.

I had never been a flirt before my marriage, and during it was oblivious to such games.

Not that there was anything overtly sexual about Teddy's remark, but I just stood there with a silly grin wondering what he had in mind. I know what I had. As it turned out, not for my beauty or charm (damn) but on account of my specialised knowledge.

'I believe you know all there is to know about Dr Charles Burney.'

I was about to dismiss such a claim with a disingenuous 'Oh no, no,' when we were distracted by the arrival of two more guests, colleagues of Felix, who were presented to us. The man, tall, lean and with large liquid-black eyes was from Goa and his companion was his short, pretty blonde German girlfriend. I did not catch their names but smiles and general small talk covered that lack.

Shortly afterwards we were all invited into the kitchen-diner to dip into dishes of Bajan cuisine. Toya had remembered my preferences, and provided me with extra treats, labelled 'Vegetarian – for Julia!' while the others ate fish with their cou-cou. Teddy and I found chairs close together, and ledges to park our glasses on while we balanced plates on our laps and ate.

He explained what he had in mind that involved me.

'Toya was telling me about her thesis on Dr Charles Burney,

and how you helped her with the research. I had known of him, of course, you can't read a book on music history without coming across him. Usually later writers refer to him only to dismiss his claims,' he laughed. 'But then I started to look into his work, particularly his writings about the music of his own time.'

'His European tours,' I nodded.

'Yeah. That gave me the idea – crazy, maybe, of reconstructing one of those tours. What do you think about taking an orchestra, a fairly small one, to Italy, in his footsteps?'

'The 1770 tour? Wonderful, sounds brilliant!'

'Well, this is where you come in. When Burney was there, he commented on the music he found in various places, and I'd like you to help me plan the tour and provide a little explanation before each concert, saying what Burney thought of the music in each place. Would you come with us?'

If he had asked me to go down a mineshaft I would eagerly have done so. 'I'd love to,' I gushed.

'Well, I have made arrangements with my contact in Naples, and he is handling matters there. I am putting together a group of musicians – friends, former students of mine, people I've worked with before – to make it happen. We shall go to four of the main places in Italy visited by Burney and play the appropriate music at each place. The programme is in draft form, Toya's been helping me. She was going to come with us and do the narrating.'

He stopped and breathed heavily, perhaps thinking how to phrase his next remark.

'There's just one big element of this that might put you off.'

I doubted it.

He continued, 'I'm hoping to televise it. There's a TV

producer I've spoken to, and she's really keen. She would put together a series of programmes about how the orchestra came together, went around the venues in Italy and played what was appropriate. She would consult you on all the historic background material and you would provide the voice-over and introductions. Of course she would need you to, sort of, audition for it, but only to check you would be right for what we had in mind. We did think of asking Lucy Worsley, but then Toya said she thought you would be perfect.'

I stood there open-mouthed. Certainly, I must have looked dazed, and nodded in a non-committal way.

Then I thought of Toya, the obvious choice for such a project.

'You said Toya "was going to"?'

'Ah, bit indelicate that! Let me have a word with her.'

He slipped off to where Toya was carrying trays of food around the groups of guests.

What, I wondered, was the mystery behind Toya not being able to go? I should have guessed.

After a few moments of conspiratorial whispers, a giggling Toya broke away from Teddy, put down her tray on a nearby coffee table, and joined Felix in the middle of the room. She took both his hands in hers and the young couple smiled at each other. Then Felix announced to everyone,

'Please, can I have your attention. I just want to say that my darling Toya has given me the best birthday present ever. She has agreed to marry me, and we want you all to come to our wedding!'

CHAPTER 2

I SPENT THE EARLY SUMMER finishing the book on the Burneys I had been working on ever since leaving London for the country. Then in June I had to take a long and boring flight to the USA to attend and speak at a conference. My interest in it was mainly to promote a previous major work of mine, a new edition of the plays of Frances Burney, published with extensive notes.

After that, during the warmest summer months, I set about researching the 1770 tour of Dr Charles Burney to Italy. There was more to it than I imagined, and I felt something like Burney himself did when he began to research his major work:

"The prospect widens as I advance. Tis a chaos to which God knows whether I shall have life, leisure, or abilities to give order."

However, it felt good to have a purpose because it was

something significant to do now. I had completed my other work and faced the prospect of joblessness when this tour was over.

I found that Burney's reason for undertaking his arduous journeys to Germany, France and finally Italy, was impressively scholarly. He had set his mind on writing the definitive History of Music from the ancient classical world to his own time, finding that most that had been written before was stale and derivative. He wanted to find original material and well-supported evidence. As he put it himself in a letter to David Garrick, the theatre director, of his two main purposes:

> "the one was to get, from the libraries to the *viva voce* conversation of the learners, what information I could relative to the music of the ancients; and the other was to judge with my own eyes of the present state of modern music in the places through which I should pass, from the performance and conversation of the first musicians in Italy".

While finding out all I could about Burney's tour, I bore in mind that my job would be to present all that was relevant, but briefly and entertainingly. There would be two audiences: the narrow one of the music fans and scholars present in the auditoria awaiting the performances, and the wider one of a television audience who may know nothing about any aspect of the music and needed to be sufficiently engaged to keep watching and not switch channels.

My previous experience was restricted to rooms or lecture-theatres of students prepared to sit still for an hour at a time in order to absorb sufficient information to pass exams without exerting much effort.

Interactive seminars and tutorials were more stimulating for me, but neither the concert audience nor the television one would be involved in that way.

I really enjoyed the research needed to produce the work required, using Ronald's flat and the British Library when necessary.

On the hottest days I walked round to Hampstead Heath and took a dip in the ladies' bathing pond, drying out by lying on a towel on the grass while reading a paperback novel. Twice I even took myself to Brighton for the day by train to smell the sea air, and once drove into Epping Forest for a jog among the trees.

One afternoon, just as I was tiring of my studies and considering taking another walk on the Heath, Teddy rang to invite me to a planning meeting. All walks were on hold as I returned avidly to the books to be sure I knew enough to sound confident at the meeting.

When the day came, I went by Tube south of the River, always an adventure for a North Londoner, and took a taxi from Waterloo to Teddy's terraced Edwardian house. He met me at the front door and took me through to the studio between his house and his neighbour's.

The studio was a large open space, formerly a motor showroom when cars were small and several could fit into the area. Now it served as a practice and rehearsal room, sufficiently spacious to squeeze in a chamber orchestra and certainly a quartet or two.

Mounted on the walls were shelves of music and DVDs of performances. Music stands littered the corners along with

stacking chairs. A grand piano and an undecorated harpsichord took up space on one side.

One corner of the room was screened off and housed a
table and chairs, with a small kitchenette forming a working
area. There were two people already seated at the table,
with papers and steaming mugs of brown liquid in front
of them.

'Right, Julia. Meet the team. This is Jackson Coen, our
principle violinist — the orchestra leader — and here's Liz,
Liz Philips, the head of the TV production company filming
the tour. Team, this is Julia. Coffee?'

I nodded to him and smiled in greeting the others. Jackson
stood and formally shook my hand. 'Ah, Julia, our consultant
academic. Pleased to meet you.'

Liz gave a simple slight handwave and smiled 'Hi!'

My first impression of Jackson was of a man who exuded
self confidence. In his fifties, he had once perhaps been handsome, with bright intelligent eyes, but the bags under them, a
purple-red complexion and yellow-grey teeth spoilt whatever
looks he might have had.

Liz was slightly younger than me, barely out of her twenties, and braved the world without cosmetic advantages. With
her fair hair drawn back into a simple ponytail, and wearing a
tracksuit and trainers, she looked more like an athlete than a
media type. But then, what did I know? I had seen only
personalities and actors in front of the cameras, not those
behind them.

Teddy produced my coffee and his from a freshly brewed
filter jug, adding milk, 'No sugar, thanks,' and sat down with
us to start work.

'Right. So far, this is where we are. We have most of the

orchestra assembled – I'm just waiting to hear whether a couple of them are still available.

Peppe, Giuseppe, is our agent, a sort of impresario, over in Italy and he's been arranging all our transport out there, plus the venues and the accommodation – and the publicity, of course. Pretty useless if we play to empty halls!

Peppe's brother Fabio will be with us once we get to Italy. We've made progress with the music academies there, so at least there'll be some professional attention.'

'That's thanks to Teddy knowing most of the top conservatory people there, that's why,' commented Jackson generously.

Teddy smiled, 'Well, yes, it certainly helps. OK, first, will you be bringing anyone with you, Julia – a partner?'

Ouch! Going with David would at one time have been as natural as breathing. He would have treated it as a great holiday. Going alone seemed suddenly pathetic and sad. I smiled bravely.

'No, just me. Oh, and I'd better tell you now, I'm vegetarian.'

'Don't worry about that, so are many of us. Me included. Now Liz, you're bringing your team. Four altogether with you, yes? And Jackson, anyone? Mimi?'

'No, just me.'

'Right. Now, down to brass tacks – the music. Oh, first thing, Julia please make a point of mentioning that the instruments we'll be using are either genuine authentic instruments of the period, or modern copies of those. It is important to stress that we are going for the closest simulation of the experience of Dr Burney in 1770. No point doing all this and then belting out the music on instruments more suited to Mahler!'

'OK, I'll be sure to make the point.'

'I'll need some background with that,' said Liz, looking pointedly at me. I nodded, and made a note on my mobile phone.

'Are they really expensive instruments?' she asked, this time consulting Teddy.

'Some of them, very,' he said. 'Insurance can be hellish, but we're using especially secure and air-conditioned transport for them all the way, so that should help.'

'Bloody hope so,' muttered Jackson. 'Mine costs a mint.'

Teddy now addressed me specifically: 'Right, Julia, the others know this. When Toya was advising us, she made the great suggestion that we cut down the number of Italian towns visited by Charles Burney to four: Milan, Padua, Rome, and finally Naples. How does that sound to you? It's all arranged in those places, so I hope you won't disagree!'

'No, they're fine. All except for missing out Bologna.'

'Why so?' asked Teddy with real interest.

'Well, it is there that Burney met the fourteen-year-old Mozart, plus the great *castrato* Farinelli. And, I know she wasn't a musician, but it is a shame to miss out the chance to mention Laura Bassi too.'

'Who's she?'

'A scientist. Pretty terrific for those days. Burney had just published a pamphlet about comets. He was into astronomy, so he really enjoyed being able to talk scientific stuff with her.'

Teddy nodded, 'Point taken. Perhaps we could do something about that in the television version, rather than on-site?'

Liz agreed, 'Sure. We'll use studio pictures of Mozart and Bologna. I'll look out for that science woman, Laura Bassi? She sounds interesting.'

Teddy then looked around, mainly at Jackson and me.

'Now the programme at each place. Have a look at that.'

He distributed sheets of paper to each of us on which were draft programmes of music, each headed by the name of the city.

'Well, what do you think? Of course, once we get going with rehearsals, we may cut some of this down a bit – and it'll partly depend on how long Julia you will be speaking for.'

'I'll talk for as long or briefly as you want. Let me take this home and I'll check that all these pieces were actually heard and commented upon by Burney, or at least could have been. And that none was composed later than 1770!'

Suggested music programme for the proposed tour of Italy

Milan

- *JC Bach, symphonies – opus three, opus six?:*
- *Traetta, arias from operas;*
- *Sammartini, Sonata for three strings x 2, also Symphony in C maj;*
- *Monza, Symphony and arias from Act One 'Achilles in Sciro'.*

Padua

- *JC Bach and Sammartini again;*

- *Sacchini, 'Salve Regina', and opera music;*
- *Tartini's 'Devil's Trill' sonata;*
- *Vallotti, 'Lamentation of the Prophet'.*

Rome

- *JC Bach, Sammartini, Tartini, Sacchini's 'Salve', and Traetta again; plus some Alberti harpsichord*
- *plus Stradella, oratorio arias and parts of Concerto Grosso*

Naples

- *Sammartini, Tartini, Sacchini, Bach again;*
- *plus Jummelli, two duets;*
- *Piccini, orchestra and voices.*

'That's great, Julia. Jackson, what do you think? Like them?'

'I do, and particularly the "Devil's Trill" – I can play the pants off them with that one. Some of the others I'll have to hear first on YouTube. I suppose you can get all the scores?'

'Yes, leave that with me. Now Liz ...'

'Looks good – of course I don't know what these all refer to, but it seems a diverse enough selection to interest the viewers. Rarely heard, authentic sound, all that goes down well.'

She paused, and looked around.

'Of course, we'll have to mock up this meeting — do it all over again — and have it filmed. Can we do it this afternoon? My people are ready to turn up with all their kit.'

Teddy looked round, we all nodded – me with a certain trepidation. If I had known, I'd have worn something smarter, had my hair cut, taken more care with the makeup …

'I'll give them a call. They'll soon fix up the lighting and so on. Do you mind if we use the bigger space? This is a bit too cramped.'

'Sure, no problem. Any questions anyone? Julia? Jackson? OK so far?'

We again nodded our agreement. Liz was now in control. She looked at me, 'Just repeat what you said here a few moments ago, that'll be fine. Teddy, you'll have to take these programmes back and give them out to us again. And,' she looked round at each of us, 'it's just you three. I won't be appearing.'

With a chuckle Jackson handed back his sheet to Teddy, and I did likewise.

'Right, then. Time for lunch. Pippa's cooking up some-thing Italian to put us in the mood!'

CHAPTER 3

I TOOK THE PROGRAMME home and at once returned to work in Ronald's flat, adding more books to the piles I had already amassed on Charles Burney. I had to read whatever I could about those composers on Teddy's programme list and to research the difference between period instruments and those of today. Teddy would no doubt help, but I needed to consult some music historians. I began making a list of such experts who taught at the music colleges in London.

It took until the evening before I got over the excitement of having been filmed. It seemed so odd to repeat the words of the meeting which had taken place just before lunch and remembering what I had said earlier.

Liz seemed happy enough with my voice. She said it carried well (years of lecturing), and I managed not to shake with nerves or laugh too heartily when I noticed a camera pointing at me.

Jackson had been annoying, adding new jokes and comments. We had to undergo several repetitions of sequences so that these intrusions could be edited from the final 'take'. Teddy was even more charming and authoritative than during the original meeting, but that was an advantage. It made it seem that we knew what we were doing.

When I began to concentrate on the names on the programme several things struck me. One was that I had heard of so few of them before. That was not unexpected, as my interest in classical, or rather in this case baroque, music was relatively new. It was Toya who had initiated me into its beauties.

What mainly stood out in the list was the absence of any woman composer. While I had read that there had been two Italian women of renown a hundred years previously, Barbara Strozzi and the nun Isabella Leonarda, it was striking that there was no woman, or none of note, in the Eighteenth Century.

I knew from literature that the social pressures were so great against women doing anything to professional level that few of them did. Even Mozart's gifted sister, Nanerl, had to give up her musical career on reaching marriageable age – the year before Burney's tour.

I began to burn with indignation and distracted myself for an hour or two researching women composers and musicians. It seems that since the Eighteenth Century there have been many remarkable women composers. Not that you would know that from the repertoire of most of the major orchestras in the world today.

Next morning, I resumed work on Burney, and where the good doctor did not provide an opinion on one or other of the pieces on the programme, I was reduced to writing biographical notes on the composers, and fill in with general Burney comments.

I worked diligently over the summer, but at times my concentration was interrupted by thoughts of David, feelings of bitterness, or simple regret. Sometimes I wondered if I had over-reacted. Was having an affair really so terrible, or so important for a man? Could he not love two women at the same time? Was I cutting off my nose to spite my face by leaving him? Did I not still ache for him? God, what a mess.

I decided to take a short break and, at her long-standing invitation, visited an old widowed college friend. We stayed in her Cornish holiday house near Falmouth for a glorious week. We walked, took river trips up the Fal, read novels, and bathed in the late summer sun on loungers in the little patio garden.

By September I had assembled a set of narratives of sorts and needed to try it out on Teddy and his musicians. That coincided with an invitation to the first rehearsal of the orchestra.

We assembled at mid-morning in the Neville Marriner Rehearsal Room in the crypt below St Martin-in-the-Fields, the famous church in Trafalgar Square, central London. A dozen musicians gathered together, although I did not count them.

Liz and her television production team were already there, trying out lighting and camera positions, and moving around a giant silvery circular screen which apparently reflects light. Teddy was in his element, organising everyone in a gentle-manly and good-humoured way.

Once the chairs and stands were laid out in the right orchestral order and everyone was ready, Liz asked the players to leave the room and walk in again, carrying their instruments and music, as if for the first time.

It seemed silly and artificial, but the players took it in good part. Many of them were used to this procedure.

I and a handful of others stayed behind in the rehearsal room, and were signalled by Liz to remain silent during the filming.

The players filed in, chatting nonchalantly among themselves until most seats were taken. Then they arranged music on their stands and began the tuning up. At that point Liz called out 'Cut!'and everyone froze.

'Sorry, not satisfied. That didn't work,' she explained. 'Everyone out again, just players please. Take your instruments and music and do it all again. You were fine, it's us who didn't get it right. Sorry about that.'

This time it seemed to go smoothly. I was given a reading-stand near the centre at the front, with my back to the orchestra and facing an imaginary audience. In fact, I was not called on to do any narrating, just to test sound levels, as Teddy wanted only to run through the whole draft programme of the full orchestral works. Duets and trios would wait for another time, as could the operatic and other vocal pieces. The singers were spared this run-through.

Each piece was first played with the conductor's occasional interruptions, as Teddy called for certain elements to be repeated with a different emphasis of phrasing, timing or dynamics. Once the piece had come together more or less as he wanted it, it had to be played right through, while Liz timed it with a stop-watch. Liz's team followed all of this without comment, the three men just moving quietly around with furry-headed microphones or shoulder-carried cameras, the sounds and instructions from Liz playing through their headsets.

I was fascinated, never having experienced a professional orchestra in rehearsal before, and was amazed at how they all kept together, sounding as one organism rather than disparate parts.

They knew when to synchronise bowing and for how long to pause. The orchestra made what, to me, sounded like perfect music at each first playing, but even I recognised the improvements after Teddy had asked for changes. I noticed slight head movements as the players looked up from their scores at either Teddy or Jackson.

When I listen to a piece of music on YouTube played by one orchestra, and then the same piece by another, I am amazed at how different the two versions can be. Now I marvelled at how the conductor's interpretation can make such a difference, just by a few gestures of his baton and hand. The orchestra followed exactly his requests for pace and volume, and his pointing at various people helped them to know when to start playing their part of the piece. My involvement in this event made me concentrate as never before on the mechanics of orchestral music-making.

Then when Teddy and a couple of the others brought the harpsichord to the front of the stage and he both played and conducted seated in front of its keyboard, I was super-impressed.

We stopped for a short lunch break. Some people went off to buy food in the café in the crypt, we others grouped ourselves in casual combinations around the room.

Someone from each of the groups went into the kitch-enette to make coffee and tea for themselves and their friends, others poured liquids from thermos flasks, or just slugged water from plastic bottles.

I quietly chomped my hummus and lettuce sandwiches and listened to the players' chatter in the group I happened to be in. Opposite me was a shy young woman, a dark-eyed beauty whom I had watched playing the viola.

On my immediate left was Jackson Coen and a short bushy-bearded fellow violinist, while on my right two bright young male cellists shared private whispered jokes between themselves, obviously close friends. At one point the bearded man gave up on his hoard of sandwiches and waved one towards Jackson, who had just a small plastic container of rice salad.

'Care for a ham sandwich anyone – Jackson? Oh, sorry, I forgot. Ham!'

'Ham would be fine,' said Jackson, smiling. 'It's the Irish Coen, y'know, without an aitch. Comes from the Gaelic word for wild goose. For Christ's sake, don't take me for a bloody Yid!' He and the other man then laughed.

I happened to catch sight of the young viola player's face at that moment and saw a flicker of pain in her slight frown and grimace. I was frozen in embarrassment at the casual acceptance of antisemitism just displayed.

The two cellists stopped their chatter and were looking askance towards the older men. They then both turned to the young woman, and one jumped to his feet and offered to fetch her a tea or coffee. The other then looked at me and introduced himself and his friend.

'I'm sorry, Julia. I'm Simon and this is Jude. We're both cellists and were students together. This is Naomi, who plays the viola like a dream, and you probably know Jackson and Edward.'

He was speaking rather quickly and loudly and I warmed to him and his friend at once.

The four of us then discussed a range of trivial matters, pointedly ignoring the two violinists among us.

Shortly afterwards, Jackson stood up, pulling out a packet of cigarettes from his inside jacket pocket, and declared his intention of going outside 'for a smoke'.

Half an hour afterwards, the orchestra was prepared to restart, and Teddy came over to me, smiling pleasantly and somewhat apologetically.

'You've got a sense of it now, I expect. Don't feel you have to stay as we shan't get round to hearing you today. I'm sorry if you feel you've wasted your time.'

'No, it's fine. I've enjoyed it. It's all new to me. I will go now, thanks, but am looking forward to the next rehearsal.'

Which I really was.

CHAPTER 4

THE NEXT DAY I WENT to visit Toya. She looked radiant. A tonic for any depressed spirits.

'Julia, it's so good to see you. Come and look, here's my dress.'

Looking at the photographs on her mobile of Toya posing with the most brilliant of smiles in a simple Empire-line white dress with a gauzy stole in pale violet, I felt a stab of anxiety. No, I mustn't let my cynicism cloud her sunny exuberance.

After we enthused about the wedding plans: the dress, the flowers, the hymns, the guests (oh good, Teddy's coming), I told her we had work to do. I drew out two sheets of A4 from my capacious shoulder bag and handed them to her.

'Please look over this script for me and put me right when I've screwed up.'

She made a few helpful suggestions, concluding: 'It's pretty much what I would have said, actually.'

Then she went dewy-eyed and asked me what I thought

about Felix and we spent the rest of the time extolling the virtues and general wonderfulness of her intended. What really impressed me about him was when she let slip a startling item of information.

'When he thought I was going to be involved', she said, eyes shining with delight at the memory, 'Felix offered to pay for the lot – well, all the expenses in the UK.'

'You mean for the whole orchestra?'

'Yes, stuff like rehearsal room costs, travel for the players and transport for the instruments.'

'Wow, that's generous.'

'The costs in Italy can be covered by sponsorship. The Italian government is pretty good like that, and the British Council have agreed to help. Then there's ticket sales and the television fees, so everyone should be paid and no-one out of pocket. Felix likes Teddy and wouldn't want him to go short.'

'But now you're not going …?'

'Oh, that makes no difference. Felix is like that. The only thing he asks for is that the logo of his City firm would get put in the programme. Like the other sponsors will.'

I stayed for lunch having helped her to prepare the salad. I left promptly after the meal as she had an appointment with the dressmaker for a final fitting of The Dress.

The morrow was hot and steamy as September days can be, and I took myself first to the dentist, and then back to St Martin-in-the-Fields. Descending to the rehearsal room below ground, I could hear the tuning of instruments and the trilling of scales from a couple of singers.

Inside the purpose-built rehearsal space, mercifully air-conditioned, were some of the players from the previous rehearsal, the production crew, and a couple of people I had not met before.

Teddy was there, deep in conversation with Liz, and I saw Teddy's wife Pippa coming from the kitchenette bearing a mug of something hot in each hand. These she handed to a glamorous blond woman and a slight young man in a tee-shirt bearing the legend 'Tenor … everyone else is accompaniment'. I guessed these were the singers.

The instrumentalists were far fewer in number than at the previous rehearsal: just four in all, although there was an empty stand behind the violins. The players were ready, seated in position to play. Jackson was in his place at the front and left of the conductor. Next to him was a tall scrawny man, of about the same age, wearing an appallingly bright Hawaiian shirt – all sky-blue and palm-trees, perhaps in honour of the heat outside.

Naomi was there tuning up her viola, and one of the two young male cellists from my previous lunch group (I think it was Simon). I noticed something I had been too excited to see on my first visit. The cellist was holding his bow differently from the usual position, and his cello had no long pin supporting it on the ground.

I remembered this was the authentic baroque style of instrument and playing and made a note on my phone to ask the string players questions about the difference in techniques with all the instruments at a suitable time. I needed that information for Liz.

Teddy broke off from talking with Liz and approached me.

'Glad you could make it, Julia. Today's run-through will give you an idea of what the other pieces sound like and what you might like to comment on. Do feel free to leave or stay as you wish. The next rehearsals will be more serious and nearer the time. That'll be when you will practise *your* performance. This is largely for Liz and the camera and sound people. Oh, and I like the drafts you emailed. Thank you for those. Right everyone, let's start with the Traetta. Julia, you might like to take notes, but I'll send you a list of the final choices, anyway. OK, Liz?'

'Fine, just let's take some soundings. Do a few bars and then stop, can you?'

'Sure. Right.'

He seated himself at the harpsichord, opened the music before him and then held up his hand. The musicians fell instantly silent, concentrating on the scores in front on them. The string players positioned their bows, and at the slight downwards movement of the forefinger of Teddy's left hand, they started off playing together.

They played for a few moments until Liz called a halt. After a pause, they started again at her invitation and stopped at the same place.

Pippa was still standing at the side of the room, by the blond woman, chatting quietly. I looked for the tenor, then noticed he had slipped to the back of the violins and was playing with them at a previously empty stand.

The two women replaced their coffee mugs with music scores and both studied them intensely. I sat on a chair facing the musicians, alongside Liz. Liz was intently occupied in instructing her team by studying a small monitor in front of her showing the different camera shots, and talking quietly into the tiny microphone at the end of a short lead across her cheek.

She and her technicians all wore heavy earphones with attached microphones. The two cameramen kept moving up and down and from side to side of the group of musicians. A third adjusted several microphones on stands ranged in front and moved quietly to the back of the room to work on a complicated-looking console, pulling and pushing faders, and pressing mixers and buttons.

Liz and I comprised the audience; two of us with very different reasons to be there.

After an instrumental introduction, the blonde soprano waited for her cue from Teddy, moved into the central position next to the harpsichord, and sang a few bars in a sort of talking-to-music voice, before launching into an aria at almost ear-splitting volume.

Immediately Teddy halted proceedings. He jokingly asked her to tone it down, to everybody's laughter, including (thankfully) hers, and called out a bar number from which he wanted everyone to start again. This time they all progressed to the point where Pippa joined in, in a *contralto* voice that was rich and full.

They sang the duet right through, then looked at Liz. She consulted her sound technician, sitting at the back of the room behind his console. He twiddled a bit, listening to sounds through his head-set, then nodded. Liz then turned back to face the musicians and gave the thumbs-up.

Teddy called out: 'From the top, this time note the dynamics Jackson, please. And Naomi, more from you from bars 60 to 82. Let's go', and they were off again.

During a break, Jackson and his colleague in the loud Hawaiian shirt came over to me.

'Hi, Julia. Good to see you again. What did you think of it?

They're not bad, eh?'

I agreed that they were far from bad. I looked towards the man in the gaudy shirt who was standing slightly behind Jackson's shoulder.

'Oh, yes – you haven't met Philip, have you? Wasn't here the other day; up to some skive, probably. Ha!'

'Hi Philip, I'm Julia – not a musician, as you gather. Just brought in to introduce the items and provide some context.'

'Philip and I are old chums,' Jackson slapped his shoulder. 'Went to the same school and then music college. Quite a reasonable violinist – or will be one of these days!'

Philip smiled wanly and studied his feet. He looked up shyly and said, 'Glad to meet you, Julia. You can call me Philip or Robinson. Most people tend to call me Robinson.'

'Then I shall too, thanks,' I said, embarrassed. Perhaps he preferred Philip, I should have asked. I extricated myself as quickly as politeness allowed, and went over to chat with Pippa, who was laughing with the two other singers. She introduced me.

'Hi, Julia. Freda and Vaclav, my singing colleagues. Julia here is to bring a touch of class and scholarship to our proceedings.' We all laughed.

'No, really. I'm just to spout a bit of background between the items – give the context. Explain who Burney was, for one thing, as I don't expect anyone's ever heard of him.'

'Oh I certainly have,' protested the blonde in an unmistakable accent.

'Hi, I'm Freda – the loud American one! Loud in all senses, I really must learn to tone it down in small spaces!' I warmed to her at once. 'The music history books we read in the Conservatoire were full of "Burney said this" and "Burney thought that". He was a real power in the land! Friend of Haydn and Sir Reynolds.'

'Joshua', added someone.

'Sure, and Dr Samuel Johnson, yeah? And Garrick and Sheridan, theatre people, right?'

Various affirmations, 'Uh-huh.' 'Yeah.' 'Right.'

Freda went on expansively, 'Y'know, that's what really excites me about this tour – we're gonna perform the very music the great Dr Burney would have heard. And in Italy. So cool – wonderful!'

Even Vaclav, who seemed shy and restrained, smiled broadly. Pippa then fell into hostess mode and offered more coffees or teas. We all declined, and Freda's face then fell, and almost under her breath, said to me:'I see you've met Jackson friggin' Coen.'

'Well, only a couple of times.' I was curious.

'Well, take no notice of him. He's a menace. Came on to me like an octopus one time backstage at the Wigmore Hall; can you imagine? I was about to go on stage and do my thing, and his hands were all over me. I nearly threw up in the wings!'

My imagination was momentarily exercised with the image of the middle-aged Jackson considering he stood a chance with the glamourous Freda. I must have looked amazed.

'Oh, don't mind Jackson,' said Pippa. 'He is a dreadful man, but a wonderful musician. That's why Teddy puts up with him. Says he's the best violinist this side of Vienna – apart from young Wing, whom you've yet to meet. And Edward, the bearded player, the other front desk first violinist. Oh dear, Edward and Jackson!' I looked puzzled.

She explained, 'Edward and Jackson both auditioned for a recording contract with Deutsche Gramophon, playing the Westhoff solos. Last week, I think?'

Freda nodded. 'Jackson got it, and Edward was furious. They're both really good but Edward said that Jackson only got the contract because he lied and claimed he'd been playing the Westhoffs for years. Typical of Jackson if that's true.'

'He upset Naomi with some anti-Semitic remark he made recently,' I had to add. (Why? Why stir things?) Pippa and Vaclav both shrugged, resigned, but Freda spoke up:

'Yeah, he's racist too in other ways. Says horrible things about Wing – you'll really like Wing. He's a young violinist from China that Teddy says will be a big star, but Jackson is rude to him whenever he can be. What a creep. But like Pippa says, he plays fantastically. So, honey, keep your distance from him and you'll be OK.'

I intended to do that. The practice soon resumed and I was transported by the beauty of the music and the vocal gymnastics of the singers. Vaclav the tenor came from behind his stand with the violins and sang too, with a light, bright voice that could sound tender at times and forceful at others. How clever, I thought, to double like that, violin and singing. Then I remembered that most serious music students tend to have more than one instrument they bring to music college to study. One of his instruments, obviously, was his voice. It's easy to transport but difficult, I imagined, to keep in tip-top condition. A hint of a cold and I croak like a frog.

I determined to improve my narrative to match the standard of the performers.

CHAPTER 5

THE WEEK OF TOYA'S WEDDING began with dismal weather for September – cold and darkly overcast. I feared for the Big Day on the Saturday, but by the time the weekend began, the skies cleared and a slight southerly wind blew in warm air. I had been shopping on two whole days, looking for suitable clothing for both the wedding and the week in Italy. I am one of those women who find shopping to be therapeutic. Not that I have ever had lots of money to spare, but I enjoy window shopping, especially of the upmarket stores which I hesitate to enter.

I eventually found a striking dress and matching jacket in a light buttery yellow at a price which, although I gulped at first, seemed reasonable for the quality. David was no longer around to raise his eyebrows and exclaim 'Good God, how much?'

That was for the wedding, and for Italy I bought in Hampstead Bazaar a full-length, beautifully-cut kaftan-type dress in deep plum with cream embroidery. The rich fabric swirled luxuriously as I moved in it. I felt happy with my new clothes and the shoes I bought to go with them. Fortunately, my light beige shoulder bag would go with all my clothes.

On the Saturday morning I primped myself up. Louisa nodded in approval and proffered a squirt of her precious high-end perfume.

I took the Tube from Chalk Farm to Oxford Circus, walking from there to Hanover Square. My happy excitement was dimmed slightly by finding certain tight spots in the new shoes, but all pain was forgotten when I arrived at St George's Church and was ushered into a pew in the magnificent neo-classical building. It was a new-build when Handel lived nearby in Brook Street and he used it as his place of worship.

I knew all this as I had looked it up before I came.

Handel himself had helped to choose the organ and auditioned new organists for it. As a lover of all things baroque, and especially of Handel, Toya must have been thrilled to know she could be married there. That privilege is generally only for those living in the Mayfair parish, which fortunately Felix did as he shared a flat with some colleagues in Gilbert Street. He was still on the lease there for a few months although he had mostly moved in with Toya in the Kensington flat they had bought together.

While waiting for the service to begin I looked around at the panels adorning the gallery along three sides, listing all the aristocracy who had been church wardens there since the Eighteenth Century.

Toya was far from being a snob or a social climber and I know would have been happy enough in a backstreet redbrick chapel so long as she were marrying the man she loved.

Yet here she was, marrying a charming Barbadian banker in Mayfair. Good for her.

The ground floor pews and the gallery were filling up with a mixture of music college friends of Toya and of City-worker friends of Felix. Who was which was hard to tell, as both groups wore similar clothes, either dressed-up and blingy, or dressed-down and hipster.

At the front I could see the backs of Felix and his brother-in-law Leon alongside Adèle, who was stunning in a colourful Caribbean dress. The two men looked dapper in well-fitting grey morning suits. Other people who were probably more of Felix's relatives filled the right-hand front pews, some in West Indian costumes, others in designer chic.

On Toya's side at the very front there were just one or two people, presumably relatives, but unknown to me. The pews behind the bride's family were filled with young excited people including one or two former students of mine. When our eyes met, we smiled broadly at each other. While I was looking around, I could hear music being played live by a small group somewhere over to the side at the front, out of my sight. I recognised the 'Gabriel's Oboe' piece from the film *The Mission* and sat back with eyes closed dreamily to enjoy it. Suddenly a voice nearby jolted me alert.

'Hello, mind if we sit here?' There were two smiling, well-dressed people standing between the pew end and the official usher; Teddy and Pippa.

'Hi, yes, please do. There's plenty of space.'

I shuffled up quickly as far as I dared encroach on the space of the young man beside me, and the two musicians crammed in. I drew in the scent of Teddy's expensive cologne and felt a warmth of pleasure, probably producing a blush.

The young man, whose shoulder and thigh I was now pressing, grinned at me in a friendly way. My happiness was complete. Apart from not having David beside me. The old David, the one I thought I could trust.

The instrumentalists finished as the organ struck up 'The Arrival of the Queen of Sheba', and we all craned round to catch a glimpse of the bride. The Queen of Sheba herself could not have looked more resplendent. Toya arrived in her full-length white Empire-line dress with a voile stole in pale violet draped across her back and over her arms. Her hand was over the forearm of a beaming grey-haired white man in rumpled morning suit. The man, I assumed to be, was the jazz-playing father whose own wife had brought Toya up. Toya's biological mother had been too busy being a successful business-woman, owning and running the hotel that employed the musician-father.

Toya and her father led a small cohort of young women up the aisle, all dressed alike in pale violet empire-style dresses colour-matching the bride's stole. Toya's long straightened Afro hair was piled up in an elaborate construction and dressed with flowers, pale purple and white, reproduced in the ones she held as a bouquet. She positively glowed, and Pippa and I exchanged smiling glances. I think a tiny tear may have trickled down my cheek. Could I be so sentimental?

After the service, we waited for the official photographs, and many unofficial ones by friends, to be taken on the church's spacious colonnaded portico. Then, while some of the congregation dispersed, I joined the other invited guests and followed the bridal couple across the road and briefly in the direction of Oxford Street before we turned left into Brook Street.

Teddy and Pippa walked alongside me as we braved the passers-by gawping at this party on foot in our wedding finery, until we reached Claridges Hotel. Once inside, we lined up to congratulate and shake the hands of Felix and his brother, and we women embraced the bubbling Toya with every expression of good wish for her happiness, while the men in the party kissed her on both cheeks. 'You're a bloody lucky man,' someone called out to Felix, while 'You look so beautiful, darling!' was directed to the bride.

We stayed together for drinks and canapés in what is called the French Salon until invited to be seated in the Drawing Room. I found my place on a chart and joined a table with a few giggling students already seated. I wondered who would take the remaining seats at our table set for ten. Then a voice spoke from over my shoulder.

'Why hello, there Julia. I didn't see you at the church.' It was Jackson Coen, all attired in morning suit and accompanied by a heavily made-up woman with an elaborate wide-brimmed hat. 'This is my wife, Mimi.'

I smiled, she barely did.

'No Mr Deane with you?'

'No, we've separated.' Not that it's any of your business, I was tempted to add, but did not.

'Oh well, never mind. I see you've got Philip Robinson sitting next to you. You remember – him with the bright shirt? You can chat about Italy together. Now where are we, next to these lovely young ladies, I hope?'

He and Mimi the Hat moved off to find their places. Just then the tall thin musician I had met at the rehearsal when he was wearing the gaudy Hawaiian shirt, appeared and took his seat alongside me. He was in sober dress, thank goodness.

'Hello,' he said, shyly. 'I'm one of the violinists going to Italy, Philip Robinson.'

'Yes, I remember. Hello. I didn't know you knew Toya?'

'Yes, I know her from the Royal College of Music. I teach there part-time. She was one of my better students in her undergraduate days. But my wife knew her better than I did. She was her keyboard tutor and she and Toya always got on well.'

I waited for him to explain the absence of the wife, but he concentrated on the printed menu sheet and said little. I made desultory conversation with the young woman on my left, a PA from Felix's city firm. We had little in common and she was not forthcoming. Before the food was produced and after the waiters saw that our flutes were suitably refilled, were the usual speeches by best man and bride's father, amusing enough and mercifully brief, with several toasts in rather good champagne.

The food courses were produced and enjoyed, although conversation somewhat wanting. Distance and background babble made it difficult to converse with the other people around the table. However, over desert, Robinson leant towards me and spoke quietly and hurriedly, as if I would be bored or dismissive if he had taken more time.

'My wife left me. In the New Year. You see, I'd lost quite a bit of money. Well, all of it actually. Some stupid investment scheme.'

He paused to draw in a deep breath, and then cast a look across the table toward his colleague, who was at that time laughing with the bubbly student sitting next to him. The Hat, on his other side, was staring into space. Miserable Mimi.

'Jackson led me into it, and then he pulled out just in time.

But I didn't see the crash coming, and lost everything – house, savings, the lot.'

'Oh, I'm sorry. What bad luck.' 'Idiot', was left unsaid. I wouldn't trust Jackson with money for chips, let alone an investment scheme. But I looked at Robinson's sad eyes and hang-dog expression and actually felt a pang. He mistook my sympathetic expression for interest and droned on.

'The worse thing was Mandy leaving. She couldn't take the strain any more of not knowing how we were going to cope. A musician's life is pretty precarious unless you're under a contract, which few of us are. We'd been married for over twenty years ...'

With a mounting urge to change the subject, I turned to my left to the young City woman with the bored expression. Suddenly she starting waving her arms around in a fit of choking.

Blimey, how do you do the Heimlich manoeuvre? I settled instead on slapping her vigorously on the back of her expensive jacket. She spluttered and coughed, flapping her hands in an effort to stop my assault. She thanked me, laughing embarrassedly and swallowed water proffered by another attentive guest. By that time Philip Robinson was preoccupied with adjusting the amount of cream in his coffee. I did not return to his conversation.

During the meal a quartet of young players had been entertaining the assembly with quiet background music. With speeches and meal over, we all stood and moved back into the French salon, now transformed into a medium sized ballroom.

A student string quartet, with a fifth player on an electric keyboard adjusted to harpsichord mode, played a medley of baroque dance pieces, with the dance-teacher from the Royal Academy of Music explaining the steps and formats. At first one or two of the guests gamely joined in, then others saw it was fun and soon the laughter-level freed inhibitions and more took to the floor, with Toya and the bridesmaids really looking the part in their Jane Austen-style dresses.

After a time, delicate minuets and gavottes were replaced by more robust English country dances. I tried a few numbers, as far as my dress and painful shoes would allow, until afternoon tea was announced. Toya and Felix left to change into more casual dress ready for the disco which would follow. Along with some of the other guests no longer in our twenties, I gave my apologies and slipped away.

CHAPTER 6

THERE WAS ONE FULL REHEARSAL of the music for the four concerts two days before our departure. It took place in the Britten Theatre at the Royal College of Music. We were to be there by ten in the morning and expected to be finished by late afternoon. I arrived in good time and was greeted warmly by Freda. Liz waved, preoccupied. The three of us sat in the front row of the auditorium, staring up at the stage which held chairs, stands and microphones.

The production people must have been there since early morning, and the technicians were sitting around at the back of the auditorium waiting for the action.

At ten past ten, just two of the players walked onstage, Simon and Jude, with their cellos and music, and settled themselves behind their stands, chatting to each other, and throwing glances offstage towards the entrance in the wings from which they had come.

Freda murmured, 'Something must be up.'

After a few more minutes Teddy appeared, stopped for a

moment to say something to the two players on stage, and walked up to the front, addressing us, the three women seated in the stalls.

'Terribly sorry about this delay. There's a spot of bother in the Green Room. Some of the players are refusing to come out until the issue's settled. Talk of union action.'

Liz asked directly and with a trace of annoyance, 'What's the problem? I thought they all got on with each other. We've been here since nine o'clock.'

'I'm sorry, Liz. It seems that Jackson has ruffled some feathers. Nelson, the bass player ...'

'The black guy?'

Teddy crouched on his haunches, the better to talk confidentially. The three of us jumped out of our seats and approached the stage.

'Yes, good man, very popular. Unfortunately, his son is up in court this morning on a drugs charge.'

We turned to each other with furrowed brows and open mouths. Then Teddy continued, 'Terrible business. Drugs that Jackson apparently introduced him to, or rather his son did. Seems that Jackson's son and Nelson's son would take drugs, cocaine, when the two boys were supposed to be practising together in Jackson's house. They're in some rock band or other. Jackson left it lying around. Apparently he takes it himself. I didn't know that and you can imagine I'm really pissed off with him about it.'

'Oh God, I'm so sorry – for Nelson and his son,' said Liz.

'Nelson's boy dropped out of our music college to join Jackson's lad and a couple of others in this group. This morning Nelson blamed Jackson for having led his boy into trouble, and Jackson said some pretty ugly racist things to him. That's when the others backed up Nelson and are demanding Jackson apologise before they'll play with him. God, I could do without this right now.'

He ran his fingers through his thick main of hair and creased his brow with worry.

Just then Jackson appeared, leading out the players, including Nelson. The party approached and stopped only when Teddy stood upright and turned to face them. Jackson then spoke in a loud, dramatic way,

'Sorry, Teddy. Didn't mean to cause World War Three. And yes, Nelson, mate, I am truly, really truly, sorry for saying what I did and I take it all back and I hope that young Ben walks free this morning and no more action is taken. OK now? Can we play?'

Everyone turned to watch Nelson's reaction to this so-called apology. Fortunately, the man had the good grace to control his obvious anger and simply say:

'Yeah, all right… Teddy?'

'Good show. Thanks Nelson. OK everyone, let's get to work. I'll just say one thing – that racist comments, or anything similar, from anyone, will not be countenanced in my band. So that's a warning, right Jackson?'

'Understood, Maestro' said Jackson, with something of a smirk.

I had thought that bitching and backstabbing were confined to academia, but now see it is universal. Drugs, though. That's serious. How do musicians play when under the influence? Poor Nelson, trying to concentrate with this going on in his family.

I was abruptly shaken out of my reverie when I realised

that the whole orchestra, and Teddy, were set up and watching me.

They were waiting for me to do my introduction. I should have been on stage, so I flew up the steps, and took my place centre-front, facing Freda and Liz. The technicians and camera-men made a gesture of 'Go'. I steadied my knees, took a deep breath to relax the shoulders, and spoke my lines. After this, and much relieved, I returned to the stalls.

Liz was happy with the footage of the rehearsal, and discussed with the company whether to include any of the preceding argument. Despite it presenting a slice of human life behind the scenes, there was a near-unanimous decision not to.

That was it. Off to Milan.

CHAPTER 7

I TOOK MY WINDOW SEAT on the British Airways morning flight to Milan, slightly annoyed that my view was mostly of the aircraft's wing. I shoved my backpack under the seat in front and buckled up, hoping the massively obese man waddling up the aisle was not destined for the seat next to mine. One of the transatlantic crossings earlier in the year had been an ordeal, as I was sandwiched between two people with the physiques of outsized sumo wrestlers. I had been scarcely able to move and getting up and into the corridor for comfort breaks on the long flight was blood-chillingly ghastly. This time, however, behind the man-mountain appeared the smiling Freda. Freda, the American soprano, shuffled into the centre seat with Naomi, the viola player, taking the aisle seat.

Naomi appeared quite nervous, fussing about her handbag and jacket, until Freda, a seasoned flyer, reassured her. After bundling her own goods under the seat in front, Freda helped Naomi do the same with hers. Once airborne, Naomi appeared more relaxed and she and Freda enjoyed a few private jokes. Then Freda turned to me,

'Hi Julia. How are you feeling about this trip? Kinda weird, isn't it, travelling with a bunch of crazy music-makers?'

'It's great. I'm looking forward to it. And I think the musicians I've met are really nice people. Well, with one or two exceptions!'

'I don't need to ask you who!'

We stopped for a few moments while the airhostess mimed the drill in the event of a lack of oxygen or an evacuation.

'Teddy's a lovely guy. Have you worked much with him?'

'Not as much as I'd like to, he really is a honey. Naomi has, though,' Freda said, looking over to the smiling, nodding viola player. She went on:

'Y'know, there are three kinds of conductors in this game — not including the handful of women. There are the predatory sons of bs who use their powers, especially if they're the company's resident conductor, to get your pants off you — guys or girls. Then there are the seducers, the Don Juans, who try it on, but if you brush them off, they just shrug and grin. At least they don't ruin your careers. Then there are the gentlemen. Teddy's one of those. Wouldn't dream of exploiting his position. Not that Pippa would let him!' She finished with a good-natured laugh.

I sat there stunned. Innocent, naïve, whatever —I had no idea that such doings went on in the cultured world of classical music. Hollywood is one thing, sort of expected in a world that wraps up its storylines in sex and makes a cult of beautiful bodies.

The #MeToo campaign and studio scandals woke me up to

that. But this world of black, even white, ties, where everyone seems so sensitive and educated, was above all that, I thought. And yet why not? Although music can transcend the mundane material world, the artists who bring it to life are really living people and their world is constructed in just the sort of hierarchical and patriarchal power system that breeds sexual exploitation. I sat staring ahead, stupefied, until Freda broke the silence.

'Do you know Italy well?' she asked.

I shook my head.

She continued, 'I was really lucky. As a student I got to spend some time in Florence and Naples working on my Italian. That's where I met Frank, y'know? The guy that plays the oboe. Oh, and the violinist Philip Robinson too. They were both there for a time, at the San Carlo opera house.'

'Lucky you,' I said, meaning it.

'Well, a singer's got to be familiar with Italian. So much of our repertoire is in that language. And it's one I love, anyway.'

'I don't know Italy well. I've only been to a couple of summer resorts on the Amalfi coast since David, my husband – well, we're separated – prefers beach holidays to cultural ones.'

'Aw, separated? Wanna tell me about that? Sorry, don't mean to push.'

'No, it's fine. Well, painful actually. A few months ago, I found out that he had been having an affair with someone at work and, well, I'm not sure yet how to deal with it.'

'Do you love him? Miss him? Can you forgive him?'

'Wow! That's a lot! I'm not sure yet what I feel … '

'Say, I'm sorry honey. I shouldn't have pushed, but I've had two husbands already – yes, I know! I don't look old enough!

I'm currently looking for number three, so if you want any advice, don't come to me – or rather do, but you mightn't like it! I can specialise in female rage against the other sex ... it's quite an art. I can make Medea look like a vicar's wife!'

I laughed with her. It was easy to like Freda, despite her bluntness, or maybe because of it. She leaned a little closer to speak confidentially.

'I'm not the only serial marriage freak you know. Jackson Coen has been married three times. His present wife used to be married to that Frank, the oboist I mentioned, who sits near Simon and Jude, our lovely gay couple.'

Ah-ha, I rather thought that of the two young cellists. Then I remembered The Hat. 'You mean Mimi?'

'Yeah, you know her?'

'Only met her once, at Toya's wedding last week. So, she was married to Frank?'

'Sure was. There's no love lost there, between Frank and Jackson, I can tell you; although Mimi is no catch, from what I've heard. Looks good, I grant you – under the paint – but a gold-digger, and that voice – all high-pitched whines. And I don't think she's ever smiled once in her life.'

At this point Naomi joined in, first looking round to check that Jackson was not in hearing distance. 'You talking about Jackson? I can't stand the man. How Philip puts up with him is beyond me.'

'Well, Philip Robinson. What a drip! He hangs around Jackson like they're blood brothers. Still, I hear Jackson is kinda generous to him.'

'Really?' I found that hard to believe. 'I thought Jackson caused him to lose his money?'

'Yeah, bad investment. A few of the guys fell for it, but they all sold up before the crash – except for Robinson. I guess that's why Jackson loans him money all the time, or even pays for him. Guilty conscience. Don't ever bet the farm on one of Jackson's schemes. You'll lose your last rooster.'

A spot of stomach-churning turbulence interrupted our chat, and then drinks and food took our attention. After that Naomi and Freda discussed the finer points of music involved in the performance the following day. Before long we landed at Linate Airport and after a short wait at the counter-clockwise carousel for our suitcases to be delivered, emerged into the warm October air and were met by the coach that ferried us the five or so miles to our hotel.

We disgorged mid-afternoon at the Milano President Hotel in the centre of the old city. The window in my room allowed a glimpse of the famous gothic façade of Milan's cathedral.

Delighted and excited, my first reaction was to call out to David, to tell him to come to the window and look. A thud in my stomach reminded me that he was not here; I was experiencing this alone. A knock at the door indicated the porter had arrived with my suitcase. Sudden panic — do I tip and if so, do I have the right amount of Euros? David would have seen to that.

The pleasant young man at the door looked a little startled at the sight of my red face wet with tears. He did not wait for a tip. I quickly unpacked, found my facecloth for a quick cold splash around the eyes, reapplied my make-up and went downstairs.

Freda was in the lobby chatting with Vaclav, the tenor who doubles as violinist, and the young Chinese violinist I had heard about and seen a few times already but not spoken to.

'Hi, I'm Julia,' I said, extending my hand.

He took it and smiled

'I'm Wing, Wing Kai. Pleased to meet you. From China,' he added unnecessarily.

'Wing is Teddy's protégé' Freda exclaimed. 'It's true. He'll tell anyone — Wing's the future Joshua Bell, the violist everyone will be talking about. And by the way, his name means Glory in Chinese. Isn't that cool?'

We spent a few more minutes chatting while waiting for Naomi, then when she arrived the five of us set out for a walk around the town. We ambled along the impressive glazed arcade, the Galleria Vittorio Emanuele II, gawping at the designer clothes and shoes displayed in the windows.

'Hey, look. Someone's been busy!' Naomi excitedly pointed out a number of colourful flyers affixed to nearby walls and lamp-posts. With a picture of Teddy smiling out with an orchestra in the background, and a portrait of Dr Charles Burney superimposed, they were advertising our concert the following night. I felt a thrill of nervous excitement. Would I be up to the job? How many people will have seen these posters and flyers? What would they make of the image of an Eighteenth Century musicologist of whom few people even in his own country had heard? Would they be intrigued? There seemed to be dozens of them along every street we passed through.

We stood gazing up in awe at the Duomo, the fifth largest church in Christendom and the one most decorated with statues and gargoyles. Wing and Vaclav decided to go off on their own, and Naomi was hesitant at entering but we cajoled her into joining us. We joined the queue, paid our entrance fee and had our bags inspected by security officers.

In the Gothic interior Naomi and Freda both asked about the significance of various items, deferring to my insiders' Catholic knowledge. Freda added her own subversive comments and a couple of times we had to stifle some unholy giggles. Tired and happy, we returned to join the others for dinner at the hotel.

'Welcome to Milan and to the start of our Eighteenth Century musical tour of Italy!' Teddy stood, addressing us all. 'Let's raise a toast to our inspiration, Dr Charles Burney.'

We all raised our glasses, chanted 'Dr Charles Burney,' then drank some of the red wine liberally provided in carafes every few feet along our table.

'Now, fellow musicians and guests, let me introduce you to the most important person here. This is Fabio,' Teddy gestured towards a tall young man seated at his right. My eyes had already been drawn to him as the most stunningly handsome person in the room, discounting Teddy.

'Fabio here,' Teddy continued, 'is Giuseppe's brother and partner. Giuseppe, as most of you know, is our agent out here. He has to stay in Naples and will meet us when we get there, but Fabio has travelled up from there to meet and accompany us on our tour.'

I caught Freda's eye and we smirked, raising our eyebrows in a mutual signal of admiration at our new travel guide.

'Fabio will be with us throughout our stay in Italy,' Teddy was saying. 'If you have any questions or problems, please address them to Fabio.'

I mentally drew up as many questions and potential problems as I could while Teddy continued his speech to the assembly. I came to with a start, to hear him say:

'Your accommodation and travel plans are all in his hands,

and I think you'll agree that all is going splendidly to date. There'll be plenty of time to get to meet Fabio over the next few days. Just remember, please, we need to be at the Conservatorio tomorrow at two-thirty for a run through, and be back there again by a quarter to seven at the latest for a seven-thirty start. The instruments will be delivered straight there. We'll be using the Sale Verdi – it's a bit big – holds nearly one and a half thousand seats – but we're only using the central section. The ideal room, the Sale Puccini, with 400 seats, has a rather small stage for all of us, and anyway is being used by another ensemble.'

Afterwards, a few of us moved into the bar while others either went out or to their rooms. Teddy and Pippa invited me to join them, and Jackson Coen and Philip Robinson moved onto our table. Teddy and Jackson were both good raconteurs. We laughed and drank. I was quietly satisfied that I could enjoy this time. Without David. Ha!

After a while Pippa expressed a need to get some sleep and she and Teddy withdrew. Jackson and Philip also stood up, and after 'goodnights' all round, followed them. I felt that one more glass of red wine, sipped in the comfortable bar area, would be a relaxing thing to do while I read the emails on my iPhone. I went over to the bar and asked for another wine, offering my glass for a refill. While the barman was pouring, I felt the body of someone pressing at my back, pushing and pinning me against the bar.

'Another one? Why not leave it and come up with me? I'll order a bottle of champagne ...' The voice was unmistakable, the words laughably clichéd. The warm breath carried stale smoke and alcohol fumes.

'I thought you'd left.'

'Couldn't leave you here all on your own!'

As a hand moved up my right shoulder and down towards my breast and another wrapped around my waist I could tell that Jackson was not going to be put off easily. I pushed back at him with my elbows, but he just laughed. The barman moved away, ignorant or indifferent to what was going on the other side of the bar. I felt a sudden panic. A shiver passed through me. I picked up the full wine glass and, barely able to turn, breathed in to gather my forces.

I possessed the fine intention of making an equally clichéd gesture – pouring my glass of wine over Jackson's head. I saw the scene playing in my mind that I would then make my dignified escape with a playful laugh. However, real life intervened. Jackson must have been leaning his head forward, possibly to kiss my neck. I misjudged the distance between my fist, clutching the wine-glass, and his face. I hit his cheekbone hard, just below the left eye, my nails or the rim of the glass drawing blood. It all happened so quickly.

'Yow!' he cried, jumping backward, covering his eye with his hand. The red wine mixed with blood pouring down his face and dripping from his chin.

'Why, you bitch!'

'I'm sorry, Jackson. I didn't mean to hurt you, but really ...'

'Jackson, are you alright?' Philip Robinson had returned to the bar just in time to see the attack.

The barman had returned in an instant and held out a clean tea towel. Philip took it and applied it to his friend's face, while I backed away, appalled. Like the coward I am, I turned and fled to the lift, jabbing at the floor number and with my heart pounding through my ribcage. I ran then to my room and sat on the bed, panting with nerves and anxiety.

Would Jackson press charges for assault? Did he need to go to hospital? Were his clothes ruined by the red wine? After a few moments my panic subsided, replaced by anger that I had been the first one assaulted. I crept out of the room and made my way by the lift back to the ground floor and the bar. The barman smirked.

'No worry, Signorina. The man and his friend, go, go. He notta so bad, just a little, er, *agitato*, is all.'

'Did he mention the police, or hospital?'

'No, no! I see itta all. You *proteggi* yourself. I see thatta. No worry!'

My heart flooded with gratitude for that man's kindness.

CHAPTER 8

THE NEXT MORNING I noticed Jackson and Philip Robinson in the breakfast room, but tried not to catch their attention. While I was eating my bread roll and cheese slices, they passed my table to leave, staring straight ahead.

I noticed a blue-black lump under Jackson's eye with a small dark red scar in the middle. His eye was half-closed with puffiness. They pushed past Freda who was making her way to my table with a coffee cup.

'Mind if I sit here? Say, what happened to Jackson? D'you know?'

I told her, shamefaced at my recourse to violence.

'You're kidding? No?' She looked elated. 'That's fantastic,' she enthused. 'Just what the bastard deserved. Hey, don't beat yourself up over that, honey. You did the right thing.'

Buoyed by her reaction, I agreed to make up another little party of her, Vaclav, Wing and Naomi for a little more sight-seeing before the afternoon rehearsal. We would find a restaurant for lunch and go straight from there to the

Conservatorio. I had not hung out in a youthful group since student days. It was fun.

We wandered around the city, stopping for coffee and then ice-cream, but foregoing a visit to the Da Vinci Last Supper mural, as we learnt that tickets had to be booked months before. Then an early lunch in a *trattoria* where two of the waiters flirted outrageously with Freda, whose repartee and banter with them had the rest of us in a state of almost helpless laughter.

Afterwards I strolled alongside Wing, while Freda and Vaclav chatted together, pointing out landmarks and laughing. Wing may have been a little intimidated by me, a woman fifteen years his senior, so I broke the ice.

'Are you still at college?'

'Yes, I graduated before the summer and now am starting my postgraduate studies with Teddy. It seems strange to call my professor "Teddy"!'

'Have you always played the violin, since you were little?'

'Yes, I started when I was four. Some people say it is already too old!'

We laughed and I desperately tried to think of something else to say. 'What else do you play?'

'I don't, only violin, but I have been learning composition too. Except ...'

He stopped and looked thoughtful. I wondered what was wrong with that. Then he continued without my having to question further.

'The only bad thing is that I have Mr Coen, Jackson, who teach me this, so I don't really like it. But now I don't have to study this any more, only violin.'

That man again. I was curious to know more. Nosy, is the word.

'What was wrong with Jackson Coen? Did he fail you?'

'No, he cannot do that, because I won the prize for composition. But he was not good with me. He want me to go back to China. He say I represent the "Yellow Peril" but I am not sure what that mean.'

I desperately tried to think of a distracting subject. Fortunately, Freda, ahead of us, held back for a moment to share a joke about a poster advertising our concert on the wall beside us that someone had defaced with a feltpen, giving both Teddy and Charles Burney black moustaches. That cleared the air, and we finished by walking as a group, sometimes having to go in single file, until we reached the hotel.

We returned to our rooms to fetch our music and, in my case, script, and then found our way, thanks to map apps on our mobiles, along the Largo Augusto and the Via Filippo Corridoni to the Via Conservatorio and thence to our venue. Teddy met us and directed us to our Green Room, but drew me aside as the others went on.

'Julia, I appreciate that Jackson can be a perfect pest at times but try to refrain from blacking his eye too often if you can help it.'

He was smiling, thank goodness.

'Oh, I'm so sorry ... I didn't mean to do it.'

'Don't worry, its fine. I just like my first violinist not to look as if he has just gone ten rounds with Mike Tyson. I am sure he asked for it, and I've had words with him. He's promised to behave, but I'd steer clear of him for a bit, all the same.'

I did not need telling.

I detested the man. But not so far as wanting him dead ...

I went to join the others. After a few minutes, Teddy appeared to say that the instruments' van from London had arrived and the crates were being wheeled into the Green Room.

I watched the players as they collected their instruments, picking them out of the cubby holes in the crates, and discarding their cases around the periphery of the room.

Then we all trouped down a corridor, up some steps and through the wing onto the stage. Music stands and chairs were already in position. The players took their places, and then produced a few moments of deafening cacophony, tuning up. At a baton's tap by Teddy on the conductor's stand, all went quiet, then the oboist sounded an 'A' note which then set off first the woodwind section and then the brass and finally the strings, until all were sounding the same note.

Teddy then drew the conductor's stand forward and directed two men who I assumed had been the drivers of the van – to position the harpsichord where the stand had been at the front, and centre stage. Once satisfied with its position, he opened the lid, sat on the stool at the keyboard and assumed authority by raising his hand and achieving instant silence from everyone. The television technicians positioned themselves around the stage and when they nodded their readiness, Teddy gestured to begin.

I sat and watched alongside Liz, with her mini-television monitor, and a non-playing woman who had flown out with one of the musicians.

She was about my age, mid-thirties, with hair severely drawn back in an old-fashioned bun, and with eyes sparkling with humour and intelligence. We laughed together as one of the wind players ran in late, breathless and apologetic, then scattered all his scores over the floor. He then dropped his flute while retrieving the papers. Patted on the back consolingly by his neighbour, the oboist, he settled down and the rehearsal resumed.

My companion in laughter turned to me,

'Hi Julia. I'm Tina – Jeremy's my husband – the viola player next to Naomi. He drags me round on these tours – not that I mind one bit. My job is to act as librarian for the orchestra, supplying missing copies of music scores and to check that everybody's playing from the same edition. If one part's in a different key, there'd be chaos!'

As the band played, I ran my eyes along them, rummaging in my memory for the names of those musicians I had already met.

From the left, of the 'first' violinists I could name Jackson Coen and the bearded Edward. Behind them was Vaclav, who doubled as tenor vocalist. Back to the front 'desk' as I had learnt to call the rows of instrumentalists, were two 'second' violinists, Philip Robinson and Wing, with Pippa Albright sitting behind them, ready to slip out to sing when the time came. Then there were the two violists, Naomi and, as I had just learned, Jeremy.

Behind them were the oboist, Frank, whose former wife Mimi was now married to Jackson. Next to him was the flautist, whose name I learnt was Martin. Frank and Martin played other woodwind instruments and even brass ones on occasion.

The versatility of musicians is amazing. At the far right were Simon and Jude, the cellists.

I was never quite sure who was who as both had neat lithe

figures, jaws shaded with short trimmed beards and wore ear-studs and pastel-coloured shirts. They could have been brothers.

Behind them was Nelson, his short hair dappled with grey, playing the double bass.

As the others began the second item, the flautist, still flustered from his late arrival, rifled through his music scores in mounting panic. Everyone stopped as he gestured wildly to Tina who went forward to see what the problem was. He called out that he had mislaid the Monza symphony.

'Don't worry, Martin, I'll print out another score,' she called out as she half-ran from the auditorium. Fabio, who had been sitting unseen at the back alongside the sound technician, hurried to join her.

While the players took a break, Teddy invited me up on stage to practise reciting my introductory speech and the links between some of the pieces.

I tried desperately not to sound too school-teachery, adding what I hoped would be considered humourous comments. I can usually get a lecture room laughing, but this was altogether different, and much more difficult to gauge.

For the links between pieces, or groups of pieces, I found I remembered all that I had written, so needed only to refer to my paper when quoting from Burney directly.

One such was from his diary entry: 'Friday July 20, 1770: A private concert in Italy is called an *accademia*.'

I added a comment on *accademias* by Burney's friend, Baretti:

"We have many kinds of clubs ... where such gentlemen — as apply any way to music — assemble on fixed days to play together till they are weary, and always without the intervention of the bottle."

I looked up to receive the expected laughter for that last remark.

'Burney goes on,' I said: "The first [concert] I went to was composed entirely of dilettanti; *il Padrone*, or the master of the house, played the first violin, and had a very powerful hand; there were twelve or fourteen performers.. and they executed, reasonably well, several of our Bach's (that is, Johann Christian Bach, known as the 'London' Bach) symphonies ... But what I liked most was the vocal part by *la Padrona della Casa*, or lady of the house; she had an agreeable well-toned voice, a good shake, the right sort of taste and expression, and sung sitting down ... wholly without affectation, several pretty airs of Traetta."'

I went on to point out: 'We've just been presented with a sample of Johann Christian Bach's Symphonies, and what we'll hear now are some of those pretty airs by Traetta.'

After my stint, the singers arrived and peformed. I sat in admiration, not only for the quality of their voices and techniques in reaching high sustained notes or fast trills and ornaments, but for their ability in remembering the words, all in a foreign language, and sounding as if they were feeling the emotions ascribed to the roles.

CHAPTER 9

THE MILAN CONCERT went well. There was a good turnout in the audience of both Italians and foreigners, largely German and American, with a few Brits. Several music students from the Conservatorio sought me out as I came off the stage to ask questions, including, 'Where can I read more about this Charles Burney? And what did I think he would say about the state of music in Italy now?'

This last really shook me as I had really no idea. I flannelled a bit about Italy still being the centre of operatic excellence, although I could not think of a single contemporary Italian composer.

I was relieved when Liz interrupted to ask if she could record some short interviews with a few of the students and did not need to involve me.

It was good to hear their positive comments about the whole performance, even of my introductions. What really impressed me was the way an audience comprised of Italian and other non-English speaking people was remarkably tolerant of someone speaking a foreign language to them. I could not imagine that happening in the UK, monoglots as most of us are.

After the show we all went back to the Green Room, where the musicians packed away their instruments and placed them in their little compartments in the large wheeled bins – like outsized trolleys that chamber maids leave in the corridor while they are servicing a room.

Each of the players strapped in the precious tool of their profession. Two men in uniforms of short blue jackets with trousers of the same colour, fastened the instruments in and then inserted wedges of foam rubber to ensure nothing would move or shake during their next stage of the journey.

Teddy then called everyone to order.

'Thanks, guys. That was a very good show. Congratulations everyone – great start to the tour. Now, those who want to go back to the hotel, feel free. Others may like to come for a meal. Fabio knows a good place to eat near here, so that's where some of us are going. Please, this is important. Be in the hotel foyer by ten o'clock tomorrow with cases ready. We'll be travelling to Padua by coach and I don't want it to go without anyone, or you'll have to make your own way there. I suggest you either walk back to the hotel now, or share taxis. See you all there. Don't be late!'

'Please, sit here,' Fabio gestured to the chair to the left of his and held it back for me. I felt flattered and delighted. This was heady stuff. The two men in blue uniforms, the same who had dealt with packing and moving the instruments, arrived as we were getting seated and took the chairs to Fabio's right.

Teddy and Pippa were already across the table. Wing and Vaclav, by now good friends, took the empty chairs at the table. The restaurant was filling up with members of our orchestra, the singers and the technicians. Liz was buying her crew extra bottles of wine to thank them.

Fabio took charge in introducing me to the uniformed men beside him. 'Julia, that is John and this is Riccardo. They are the drivers of the van of the instruments.'

John and I said 'Hi!' while Riccardo stood and stretched out his hand for me to shake.

'Riccardo is my cousin,' smiled Fabio. 'He is from Napoli, but works now in London, driving for Harmony Transport. I ask always for him when the van comes to Italy.'

That made sense, I thought. Another member of the tribe – Giuseppe, the unseen boss of the enterprise; Fabio his brother; and now Riccardo, his cousin. I wondered how many more family members I would meet on this trip.

John looked tired and said little during the meal. I supposed I would have done too after driving from London overnight. He was about fifty, rather overweight and totally outclassed in personality by the bubbly Riccardo. Riccardo was tall, lean and handsome, like his cousin, but with his hair pulled back into a man-bun atop his head instead of it being thickly curled.

Fabio and his cousin shared a couple of private jokes in Italian, laughing heartily, and then Fabio turned to recommend items on the menu that he believed would appeal.

After the meal, Fabio took the lead in taking our party back to the hotel. The adrenaline was still pumping in me from performing in public, and I knew I would not sleep. So, when Fabio suggested that he and I shared a drink or two in the bar, I accepted. I may have been still married, technically, but was adjusting to my new separated, single status, and the freedom that gave me to drink with handsome men of slight acquaintance.

We laughed, and talked, and drank. He told me about his childhood in Naples, and I him about mine near Liverpool. He is a year younger than I am, and still lived in an apartment with his parents. He had had an affair, when he rented his own flat with a young woman from Sicily who was working in Naples. But, for some reason it had not worked out, and he returned to the nest. I told him about my ten-year marriage with a man whom I thought I knew, but realised I did not. The David I had loved was honest and honourable. The one from whom I parted was neither.

Fabio went quiet and put his hand behind my head, running his fingers through my shoulder-length hair.

'You know, Julia, you are a beautiful woman.'

'Oh, come on! That is such a cliché. Tall, dark Italian chats up English woman with that tired old line!' I felt insulted and embarrassed that he thought I would fall for that, and covered my feelings by laughing.

He smiled, but he did not laugh.

'No, I am sorry. It does sound ... *troppo*. But actually, it is true. Perhaps your husband forgot to say that to you. He must be *un idiote totale*. To be married to you and to let you go away — *imbecille*. Maybe you do not have confidence in yourself?'

Again I protested, but did not move. Nor did I stand up and leave the room in a dignified manner. No, I stayed, basking in the attention.

He then told me about his brother, Giuseppe, and about how he had betrayed his wife one time and she left.

'But he implored her — you say that? He not eat or nothing. She came back to him. Now they are together and he never goes with another woman. Never.'

I felt the time had come to leave. The conversation was taking a turn I did not want to pursue. I felt a bit choked and was afraid I might start to cry. The last thing I wanted was Fabio's pity. I gathered up my handbag and stood.

'Please, I come with you. To see you safe.'

I could see no harm in that. Foolish girl! Of course, at the door of my room he stood close and bent towards me for a goodnight kiss. It had been a long time since I had experienced the ambiguity of such a gesture.

I found my arms were circling him and with my encouragement, his kiss becoming more passionate. Suddenly we broke off and, as I had the card-key in my hand, I pressed it against the doorlock, which clicked.

I opened the door and we both stepped inside, resuming the embrace. He gently kicked the door shut while we were glued together, and we moved as one towards the bed.

CHAPTER 10

THE NEXT MORNING I awoke to find myself alone. Someone had obviously shared the bed ... Noooo!

My head swam with jumbled thoughts: *My God, what did I do? Was I really ... with Fabio? Fabio? Well, he's gorgeous; it was great. Thank God he used something, otherwise I could really be in the ... No, what am I saying? I'm not a kid; I'm not a student anymore, and anyway I didn't then – I've never slept with another person, only David, ever ... until now.*

Oh David, I'm so sorry! No, why should I be sorry? I'm a grown woman – yes, but a married one! What? Hell, I'm no better than David! Yes, I am. He can't judge me. He started it. If he had not been unfaithful, I wouldn't have dreamt of doing this with Fabio. Well, I might have dreamt ... Oh God, that's pathetic.

An excuse. I am an agent, a free agent. I can do what I want. Of course I wanted it. I was drunk. No, I chose it, freely.

To spite you, David? Yeah, maybe. Oh hell. I also chose to be a Catholic, and what I've done is a sin. A big one. It's actually adultery. Blimey, that and contraception – it couldn't be worse. Well, so what? The marriage is over anyway. Oh God, do I want that? David, you bastard ...

The cold water of the shower snapped me awake. I had forgotten to adjust the temperature and had to wait shivering for it to warm up. Afterwards I stepped out onto the bare floor, the bath mat out of reach, still draped over the rail. I dried and picked out a dress from the wardrobe, put it on and then stuck my legs in a pair of trousers. Stupid. Not thinking. Well, thinking too much, but not concentrating on the job in hand. I stuck some lipstick on and brushed my damp hair, then went down to breakfast.

I went through the motions of eating, and greeting people, but as though still asleep, or at least dreaming. The one clear thought I had was that I did not want to encounter Fabio. I looked around warily ... Liz, the TV producer, came and sat alongside and made pleasant small talk. At least I supposed so. One of her technicians came up and spoke to her. Was he smirking when he glanced over to me? Did everyone know what I had got up to last night? Was it written on my face, or – horrors – was Fabio bragging about it?

I turned around, my head like an owl's, as I scanned the room. Yes, there he was, over at a table in the far corner, talking seriously with Teddy and Pippa, their heads down, taking in whatever was being discussed. Then they stood up and Fabio left the room, holding a folder close to his chest. Teddy and Pippa circulated, dividing the tables between them.

'Morning Liz, morning Julia. Please be ready to go in twenty minutes. The coach will be outside and if you just leave your cases in the hall, they'll be put on board for you. It's about a three-hour journey, and we'll make a coffee stop after about an hour and a half. OK? Liz, your guys have stashed their gear in the instruments van, so they'll be with us on the coach.'

I failed to notice the countryside between Milan and Padua. The morning's conversation with myself still playing on a loop. My moods swung from chippy defiance to religious guilt, and from secret satisfaction that I could still 'pull', to deep, stomach-churning fear that David would find out.

At one moment I wanted him to do so, to be able to sneer 'See, that's how it feels'. Then I would be gripped with panic at the thought that he would then claim the moral high ground and be the one to terminate whatever relationship we still had or could have.

How could I face the Deanes, his upright, God-fearing parents? It was bad enough, in their opinion, for a wife to leave her husband, without committing adultery as well.

My own mother is different. She would no doubt laugh it off. After all, she spent the years when I was growing up having serial affairs in a hippy commune. Helena might be a respectable married woman now – but who knows how long that state could last? Hey, who am I now to condemn? I dreaded, with tears pricking my eyes, the thought that Nana Ivy, the grandmother who raised me, would hear of my one-night stand, and her silent sorrowful acceptance would be mortifying.

I was glad to be sitting next to quiet, gentle Philip Robinson, who seemed to sleep throughout the journey or stare through the window without bothering me with unwanted conversation. I felt he sensed that I did not care to chat.

Maybe I had hurt him at the wedding reception by not returning to his account of his woes. Or maybe he was simply mulling over his own problems. Now his wife had left, and he was reduced in circumstances, his daughter and her potential career in music was all he lived for now.

Somewhere he had mentioned recently that she had failed one of her exams at the music college where Jackson was a tutor, and she had had to resit it. The result would be known any day now.

I thought it strange that, while he complained about the precariousness of a musician's income, he still wanted his daughter to follow the profession. According to him, and others I had spoken to, few people make it to the top where they can command large fees; most are chasing orchestral posts or take up teaching to eke out a living. Still, maybe music is some kind of drug, or psychological condition that takes you over so that you cannot imagine life without it. Rather like me with David. Even in his absence, he dominated my life.

We got out for coffee at a roadside café. Philip and I shared a tray and a table.

'Have you heard about your daughter's resits yet?' I thought I would be neighbourly and take an interest. He seemed more lost than I did which shook me up.

'No, any day now. She's out of her mind with worry. It's only the one composition theory paper but could stop her returning next year if she fails it.'

'Did someone say that Jackson was marking it?'

'Yes, he teaches the subject and is their main theory examiner. Of course, that shouldn't make a difference – that he's a friend of mine, but all the same ...'

'You hope he's fair,' I finished off for him.

'She's so good, really very talented – just not the academic sort that can pass exams easily. She panics and then can't think straight.'

I sympathised, knowing several students that I used to teach who were like that. Although they had good A levels, they could not think creatively enough for more challenging examination questions. We mused on the misfortunes of life, and reboarded the coach. I could hear Freda causing merriment among her companions further back and wished I had been sitting nearer her. But probably in my mood, it was best I kept apart.

The hotel in Padua was in the heart of the old town, and only a few yards from the Basilica of St Anthony. As we arrived at the reception desk, Teddy quietened us to announce that a tour of the basilica would commence in about twenty minutes. The tour had been arranged by him, in order for any of us who wanted to see where the composer Tartini had been chapel master and the seventeenth-century singer and composer Barbara Strozzi was buried.

I was glad that a woman composer was being recognised, but felt in no mood for visiting holy places, even those commemorating two outstanding musicians. Freda waved across the room to me and mouthed 'You going?' I shook my head. I was annoyed with myself later as Tartini had been the object of a three-day enquiry by Burney during his brief stay in Padua. The composer had died less than six months earlier and Burney was intent on learning as much of him as he could.

I could not even be bothered to go to see his resting place. Lunch was recommended in the restaurant next door, and after freshening up in my room after the suitcase arrived, I went to it, hoping few of our party would be there.

I sat at a table on my own and was studying the menu, when a voice sounded over my shoulder.

'Hello, Julia. May I join you?'

'Jackson, of course. Not going to the basilica?'

'No, religion's not my cup of tea. Actually, I've been before. But I thought you'd have gone?'

My chance to be left alone.

'Well, I really don't feel like anything, right now. I think I've a migraine coming on.' How could I tell such a barefaced lie?

'Food might do it good.' He just didn't get it!

We ordered and waited in silence. Then in a tone replete with sincerity, he said, 'I'm really sorry about Sunday night. Didn't mean to upset you.'

'No, I'm sorry. I didn't mean to hit you. How is it now?'

'Oh, nothing. The scar will remind me not to chat up beautiful women in bars.'

I smiled feebly, but with relief. He could have had me charged with assault. I shall never do that again. Maybe he was not as bad as people made out. Right now, he seemed quite easy-going, even pleasant.

'Tonight's your big moment, isn't it? The Tartini "Devil's Trill"?'

'Yes. I love that piece. I used to find it really challenging, but I think I've got it now. It's a real show-stopper. Are you going to introduce it?'

And so our conversation went, bland and harmless. Jackson told a couple of musician in-jokes, such as 'How can you tell when a singer is at the door? They can't find the key and don't know when to come in.' Ha, ha.

I was grateful for the light tone of the conversation and

felt better by the end of the meal. I was just reassessing my opinion of him, considering him to be good company, when I remembered Wing.

'I hear you taught Wing for his degree?'

'Yes, not a bad composer, but not as good as Teddy thinks he is. Probably a better violinist, but not first rate. He's got the techniques all right — practises like a mad man. Up at five every morning just to do scales and exercises before breakfast. But no real flair, no inner feel for it, no heart or passion. Just like lots of these Chinese you know. Their way of getting on, work like hell, but all sweat and no inspiration. If I had my way, we wouldn't let them in. There are so many of them, hordes all wanting top careers in music. Like his sister, for example. Let one in and the whole bloody family follows. There'll be no room for our own kids soon.'

I was making fists with my hands until the knuckles whitened and the nails hurt my palms. Then, alerted by his mention of kids, I remembered Philip Robinson's daughter and asked if he knew the results of her resit. His face clouded.

'I'm afraid it's not what he wants to hear. She's a nice girl – went out with my son once or twice. But she's really not at the level she should be in college, not in the theory at least. I'll let her tell Philip herself – and then he'll be all mopey and a bloody pain for the rest of the week. Oh well, we can't live through our children, can we?'

'You have just one son?'

'Yes, he's done all right. Plays in a rock band. Not my sort of music, but it pays better! He and Nelson's son and a couple of other mates. They're music college trained, but prefer the youth scene. All drugs and sex. What we're missing! At least I am, you're young enough still …'

I was glad the waiter appeared for the settling of the bill. I was able to wave away Jackson's offer to pay for my meal as I brought out the Euros. Then I put my hand to my head (what a phoney!) and pretended I was in urgent need of a lie-down. I was out of there and back in my room before I could let him see how worked up with anger I had become. There was so much to be angry about, not least the memory of Nelson's son being in court awaiting sentence, for drugs, to which he had been introduced by Jackson's son. I could just see Jackson thinking it was all a bit of fun.

I really wasted being in Padua that afternoon, not venturing far from the hotel and mostly lounging in my room until the time for the late afternoon rehearsal. I realised that this was the city of the Giotto frescoes covering the whole interior of the Scrovegni chapel, but had not booked in advance and, anyway, had little inclination to enjoy myself.

That evening, in the Cesare Pollini Conservatorio de Musica, before an audience of Italian music students, teachers and members of the public, I performed my narrative. I told them how Charles Burney had spent three days in their town researching his forthcoming project, the History of Music, and attending concerts and recitals.

He had missed his hero Tartini by a few months, as the celebrated composer had died that year, 1770. Before the orchestra was to play the Tartini piece in the programme, I related the legend behind the 'Devil's Trill'. According to Burney, in a dream the composer had entered a pact with the Devil, and then heard him, the Devil himself, playing an extraordinary piece of music, surpassing anything he had ever heard before. When he awoke he tried to recapture that wonderful sound, writing the 'Devil's Trill', "but it was so inferior to what his sleep had produced, that he declared he would have broken his instrument and abandoned music for ever, if he could have subsisted by any other means".

I turned to indicate that Jackson would be the soloist in this piece. He grinned.

'Charles Burney,' I went on, 'considered Tartini to be one of the few original geniuses of his age. He said of him: "His melody was full of fire and fancy, and his harmony simple and pure. He was one of the first who knew and taught the power of the bow; and his knowledge of the finger-board is proved by a thousand beautiful passages, to which that alone could give birth." We'll now hear the orchestra play the very piece inspired by the Devil, with Jackson Coen, the soloist …'

His playing was superb, as was that of the whole orchestra. At the end of the concert, Liz signalled that all had recorded well, and the brief interviews she took of departing audience members indicated general satisfaction. I gave the after-performance drinks a miss, avoiding Fabio's eye at all times, and went straight to bed. On my own.

CHAPTER 11

THE NEXT MORNING most of us set off for Rome where we were to spend a couple of days relaxing before Friday's concert. The duo of Simon and Jude, with Wing and Naomi, formed a youthful gang led by Freda. They had opted to divert to Venice and follow on a later train. They had left by the time I went down to breakfast. I was still feeling miserable, and made more so, both by the absence of Freda (with whom I was hoping to travel). And by the memory that Venice was where David and I had planned to celebrate our twelfth wedding anniversary this year, which was also the fifteenth of our first meeting. I was joined at the table by Vaclav.

'Not going to Venice? Your name, Vaclav, have I got it right?' I asked, trying to sound cheerful. Both were stupid questions, but ice-breakers. I had not really spoken to this young man before although we had been in the occasional sightseeing group.

'Yes, you have. Same as the former President, Vaclav Havel.

And no to Venice, I've been before,' he said. 'As you've probably guessed about the name, my parents are Czech. Came to
Britain in '89. Anyway, about Venice. I had the lucky chance
to sing there, at the La Fenice theatre. Just a minor role, but it
was good for my career. Rigoletto, I was one of the courtiers.'

'Was that when Freda was there?'

'Oh no, much later. 2012. Under the conductor Abbado –
Daniele Abbado, not his father Claudio. Quite an experience.
Frank was in the pit, playing woodwind. That's where I first met
him. He put me in touch with Teddy, and I try now to be free for
when Teddy does his tours, either as a singer or an instrumen-
talist. I'm not really good enough to go truly solo with either.'

I warmed to this honest and modest young man. I say
young, I mean five or so years my junior, 30-ish, I'd place him.
I fell to thinking how cosmopolitan was a musician's life.
Exciting, but unsettling too. Hard on family life, I would
imagine.

Just then Fabio appeared at the table, distributing train
tickets for those of us who were skipping Venice. Having
managed to avoid eye contact with him for most of the day
before, now I simply blushed, or it felt as if I were. Embarrassed, certainly.

A fleet of taxis arrived to collect the non-Venice people
and take us to the station. There we duly validated our tickets
in the date-stamping machine before boarding the high-speed
train to Rome.

'Let me help.' Fabio was already manhandling my suitcase
before I could answer, tossing it on top of other cases in the
luggage cage as if it weighed almost nothing. I thanked him,
and hurried along the carriage, taking a window seat.

'Ciao, Julia. Is OK I sit here?'

I gulped, nodding feebly.

Fabio took the seat on the aisle.

'You like Padova?'

'Of course, it's lovely.' How banal. How could I say that I missed most of it through guilty reflections on our antics the night before? I had to add, 'I'll have to come again some time to see the things I missed.'

'I hope so,' he smiled. 'Then I will show you all the best places to visit. Yes?'

I nodded, non-committedly. We sat for some time in silence. I stared out of the window and then remembered the book I had packed in my shoulder bag. An escape.

Losing concentration, I stole sideways looks to see what Fabio was doing. Nothing very much, his eyes were closed. I relaxed and breathed more deeply. The warm morning sun fell on me and my book slipped from my grip as I started to snooze.

'Here. You will lose it,' he said, handing me the volume, his eyes looking into mine with amusement.

'Thank you,' I replied stiffly, hoping he would sit back into his seat again.

I tried to stay awake after that, concentrating on the features in the passing scene. It was not difficult to find the landscape fascinating, from lush plains to undulating fields and to the rugged forested mountains of the Apennines. Fabio moved a little closer to point out some of the highlights of the views as we passed, naming one or two of the small towns clustered atop hillsides or sprawling down their sides. I guiltily enjoyed the shared intimacy of those moments, and the little jokey comments we made on the supposed lives of people inhabiting these picturesque places.

The heat and brightness of the sun through the window glass, despite the air-conditioning, still made me feel drowsy. But before I could prevent my eyelids from drooping, I was vaguely aware of slowly leaning towards Fabio and could do nothing to stop it. When I suddenly awoke, my head was on his shoulder, his arm around mine and a ticket inspector was standing beside us, looking impatient.

We both jolted upright and I scrabbled in my shoulder bag for my ticket, which I found and presented for the inspector's approval. Fabio gave his, and the man left and went to the next pair of seats.

Fabio grinned at me and I could not resist smiling back. So much for will-power. The rest of the journey passed without much conversation. For some of the time Fabio went off to speak to other members of the group while I either read or snoozed sitting upright, probably with my mouth open, or gazed through the window.

Some three hours after our departure from Padua, we arrived at Rome's Termini station. We disembarked, gathered ourselves into a group, and then followed Fabio like children on a school outing as he led us out to the Via Cavour and onto a waiting coach. I must admit I felt a bit special as Fabio trundled my suitcase behind him along with his own. That will start tongues wagging ... I thought I had better dampen that risk down, so I made a point of finding a seat next to an occupied one, just in case Fabio intended joining me.

Vaclav was my companion. He and I watched Rome passing by, pointing out people and buildings of interest to each other. The coach driver obligingly took a route that passed close to the ancient Forum and the Colosseum.

I recognised the St John Lateran Basilica and was rather thrilled to see from the signposts that we were travelling along the Appian Way, albeit the New one, passing old commercial buildings and new shops, parks, and eventually residential apartments.

It seemed that in no time at all the busy streets of Rome gave way to countryside as we wound our way up the hill road, passing by Ciampino airport and the hillside town of Marino Lazio, and upwards toward the lakes.

In less than an hour from leaving the busy Rome railway station, the serenity of the blue-green waters of Lake Albano sparkled below us. The coach turned off the road into a narrow private drive, and waited at a line of bollard-posts for them to be lowered. We soon arrived at the Villa Palazzola. I had seen advertisements about the place in the Catholic journal *The Tablet*, but had not thought that secular groups like our orchestra could stay there.

We disembarked and pulled out our suitcases from the hold. Then we all stood for a time just taking in the breath-taking view. The lake lay below us, surrounded on all sides by deeply wooded banks. The feature's formation as an extinct volcano was obvious. Across the expanse of gleaming water and atop the opposite bank, the white buildings of the small town of Castel Gandolfo, where the Pope's summer residence is based, twinkled in the midday sun.

Fabio and Teddy called us to enter the building, and we dragged our suitcases over the flagged floors of the ancient monastery. We were welcomed at the reception desk by two smiling ladies. Janet, the English Director, introduced herself and Cosima, her Italian assistant, who gave us our room cards.

'You'll be the only ones here,' said Janet, 'apart from Father Hayes, who is spending some time having a quiet break. You'll see him around, but don't worry about using all the public rooms. They're all at your disposal. I hope you'll be happy here and will want to come back, with your families, perhaps, for a holiday.'

When Cosima had collected those of us in adjoining rooms, she bid us to follow as she led us through the chapel and to the foot of a stone staircase. Here, one of Liz's television technicians, a man so blond as to be almost albino, offered to carry my suitcase. I was deeply grateful, though Liz, just in front of me, shot me a look as though I had just betrayed the sisterhood with my wimpishness. She had all her luggage in a bulging rucksack on her back.

This,' Cosima informed us at the top of the stairs, 'is the new building.'

'New?'

'Only about three hundred years old, not at least eight hundred, like most of the old part. But the building itself is very historic, it goes back to at least the time before Christ, maybe two hundred years, when the Consul of Rome, Scipio Hispalus, he lived here. You see his tomb, well you do not see it but you see the symbols of the Consul, the sticks, the *fasci*, they are carved on the rock face. You see in the upper garden.'

We then trooped along the corridor, Cosima indicating each room to its intended occupant. She and I were alone when we arrived at the last room.

'This is your room,' she said, smiling and opening the door.

I went straight over to the window and was instantly enchanted. When I went back to thank Cosima, she had already disappeared round the sharp right-angle bend in the corridor a few yards from the room.

I returned to the view, gazing over the lake, taking in acres of wooded hillside. My window looked out on to the right-hand side of the lake and the hillside, with the distant shimmer of Rome beyond and far below. Beyond the crater's rim I could make out the Ciampino airport's buildings and over to the left a stretch of twinkling blue, which must have been the Mediterranean beyond Ostia. I could feel the smile on my face widening at every aspect.

In the room was a single bed, a desk and chair, a wardrobe and a door to the *en suite* shower room. Simple but sufficient – and with such a panarama I was drawn repeatedly to the window. Eventually I tore myself away and returned along the corridor, with its strange sharp bend half way along. Others emerged from their rooms and together we went down the stairs, through the chapel, and along a cloister-passage. To our left was a glazed-in paved courtyard, with a covered well in its centre. Turning sharply into another passage we saw Cosima standing at a doorway, ushering us into the refectory where we sat at long tables for our lunch.

Teddy addressed us: 'Well, everyone. I hope you're all settled in. So far there have been no problems, and we're expecting the instruments' van early this afternoon. The last I heard from John and Riccardo, the drivers, they had stopped off before Rome for a short comfort-stop and should be here shortly after lunch. We're holding some food for them.'

'Where can we practise?' asked a voice.

'As we're virtually the only guests here until Sunday, you

can use any space. There are a couple of large rooms on this floor; there's the library; and a lounge upstairs in the new building; and I suggest you use the chapel for violin section work, if you want it. Otherwise, in your rooms.'

There was a buzz of quiet discussion as the musicians made arrangements with each other.

Teddy drew their attention to him as he continued: 'We'll be having the run-through on Friday morning in the conference room. I'm sure you'll find it by then. Meanwhile, have fun – explore and enjoy the Villa, its grounds and the woods around. Just ask at reception or Fabio, Pippa or me if you need anything. If you want to go into Rome, we'll arrange a taxi for you, or if you'd like to go to the town across the lake, Castel Gandolfo, we'll get one for that. The coach has gone back now and there won't be one here until Friday evening to take us all to the concert venue. Pippa and I are based in the suite known at Piazza Venezia, just round the corner on this floor. You'll see it on the way to the garden.'

After a typical Italian lunch, and a couple of beakers of the local Frascati wines, I decided to explore the grounds. I turned from the cloister into a corridor which led outside to the terrace, passing the Piazza Venezia suite of rooms where Teddy said that he and Pippa were staying.

I walked slowly around the formal gardens, laid out with low hedges and rectangular lawns. At the end, screened by trees from the Villa, were further paths around a fountain topped with a carved dolphin figure. I returned to the terrace, which now held some of our party sitting in the sun or shade, with glasses before them, chatting or snoozing.

Vaclav waved, but I did not want to sit. At the corner of the terrace furthest from the lake, I found a narrow passage. This had the Villa on one side and rough-hewn solid rock on the other, forming a shallow cliff. Above this was another building with grounds overlooking the Villa.

I made down the passage and came into a open yard, with on one side, the new wing of bedrooms opposite the cliff, on another the Villa and, in front of me, the side of what I found was the conference room, with a statue of Our Lady in a niche in the wall.

As I crossed the courtyard, I heard coming from one of the bedrooms raised and angry voices. Naturally, I stopped to listen. The sounds were of two men engaged in a row but whose voices they were I had to strain to catch. After a shouted 'Bloody hell, Jackson!' and 'Sod you, Teddy Albright!' I knew whose they were. Then a door banged and I moved swiftly away in case one or other of them saw me standing there listening.

A man I had not seen before was walking towards me. He was wearing a clerical collar with a black shirt so I guessed this was Father Hayes.

'Hello,' he stopped to say, looking up at the window where the shouting had come from, 'Someone's not very happy, from the sound of it!' I recognised at once his accent. A fellow Liverpudlian.

I smiled. 'No, just some of our orchestra having a difference of opinion.'

'There was I thinking all would be harmony and sweet accord from musical people.'

I liked him and agreed readily to his offer of a drink on the terrace.

'I'll be able to tell you more about this place, if you like.

And you can tell me about you and what your band is up to here.'

I retraced my steps along the rock-sided walkway to the terrace and we found an empty table overlooking the lake. The priest went to fetch a couple of coffees from a machine opposite the Piazza Venezia, while I admired the view and drew deep contented breaths.

Within a few minutes of conversation I learned that he was on temporary leave from a busy inner-city parish, having suffered a minor heart attack, and been ordered to rest by both his doctor and his bishop.

'I usually take no notice of the archbishop, but I do of my doctor,' he said, his eyes crinkled with humour. 'So now, what about you, what do you play and why are you here?'

I explained all and even mentioned the situation with David. His face went serious at this point, and he looked thoughtful.

'That's sad, you know. I'm sorry Julia. I know relationships are difficult at the best of times. God knows, I've seen enough suffering in my own parish. Sometimes it's better if one of the partners leaves, sometimes it isn't. But, can I tell you a story – a true one? It may mean something or nothing – that's up to you, but it seems it might just help.'

I nodded cautiously. I was curious, but reluctant to be preached at. I need not have been.

'It's about this man in Liverpool, time of the Napoleonic wars when a lot of men came back from the fighting and had nothing – no money, no jobs: nothing. This man, Joseph Williamson, had made money in trade, plus had married into the Tate family, you know, the sugar people. Big business in Liverpool that was, as you know. So he was loaded. Anyway he set scores of men digging tunnels under the city, great vaulted arches, pits and passages. Just to give them employment and wages, really.'

I nodded to encourage him to continue.

'Anyway, one day he invites all the top people in town to a dinner in one of the underground chambers. So they turn up in their finery and sit down expecting great things. But d'you know, he serves them nothing but porridge and hard biscuits – sailors' fare. Many of them get up and leave in disgust. They weren't having it. Some people stayed. Then, when the others had gone, Williamson invites the ones that stayed into a further chamber, and there, spread before them, was a feast – fine food and wine and everything! He knew who his real friends were. Great, isn't it?'

He stood up. 'Well, I've got to go now,' he said. 'It's been lovely talking with you Julia. And I'll see you around. I might even come up to your concert on Friday night!' He smiled and left me, sitting there wondering why he had told me the story of the Liverpool philanthropist.

I then shook myself. I had things to do. I had further places to explore. Returning to the yard where I had met Father Hayes, I continued to the facing wall, entered a short dark passage with storage rooms off it, and climbed a concrete staircase. It led to a small hallway with five doorways: the facing one led outside; the one to the right to a set of lavatories with a washbasin between them; the further door on the left I peered in through small shoulder-height windows to see the conference room set out for the orchestra. The other door led to a long but narrow sitting area. I walked along it to a door, and opened it. To my surprise it led to the bedroom corridor, my door being the first on the right.

I doubled back, passing the sitting area, to the hallway. This time I entered the spacious conference room, which looked as if it had once been an oratory, not as old or grand as the chapel on the ground floor. I walked around the music stands and imagined playing an instrument in here and being part of the team of music-makers, creating beautiful sounds from wood and wire and tubes. I stood in front of the empty chairs and waved my arms as I had seen Teddy do, but without knowing how it was done properly. Enough. I had more to see, so went outside across a short concrete bridge-path. A rough dark set of steps led down to the floor below, but I wanted to stay on the higher level where a paved area opened onto series of ever-narrower rough-grassed gardens.

I climbed rough broken steps from one garden area to the next and on reaching the last, and highest, turned and returned to the conference-chapel. On the way, I explored the rock cliff to our left, with the rather weather-worn fasces carved in relief where the Consul's tomb must have been. At the foot of this wall were caves with deep, dark vaulted chambers, silted up almost to their roofs. Near the door leading inside was a shoulder-high retaining wall behind which a flat, stony platform held a life-sized Madonna statue. Beyond it were several dark holes in the rock going back and down presumably unfathomable distances.

After all this exploration I went to my room to unpack. There were murmurings outside on the corridor. Never one to miss out on what was happening, I stepped out of the room.

'It's not turned up – the van.' The blond technician was visibly concerned.

'They set out at six this morning, and its only a five-hour

drive,' Liz added, with visible annoyance. 'Even allowing for a break before lunch, they should be here by now.'

Others joined us on the corridor.

'Three hours late! I've just been down and they're not here yet.'

'Let's go and see Teddy.'

'Or Fabio. He might know.'

CHAPTER 12

I FOLLOWED THEM DOWN to the reception desk. There were so many noisy members of the orchestra already crowding the area, Teddy was having to shout to get attention.

'Stop, everyone, please! I know it's all very worrying, but I rang the company in London, and Harmony Transport are getting back to me as soon as they hear anything. It seems the drivers' mobiles are just ringing out. But don't worry, the company has a tracking device on the van, so they'll soon know where it is. They probably just got lost.'

The crowd began to move back from pressing up against the desk. Some sat on the low window ledges with their backs to the courtyard. Others walked toward the corridor where there was a coffee machine, returning with small plastic containers of the liquid. One or two went outside, as if looking up the drive would bring the van down it more quickly.

I stayed on the outside of the group, having no personal

interest in the van and its contents, but as curious as the others as to its delay. Fabio appeared through the outside door, and his face was a picture of anxiety, deep furrows between those eyes which no longer sparkled with good humour and joy of life.

He moved through the group to the hinged desk entrance, lifted it and approached Teddy. They whispered together until suddenly Teddy's telephone rang with a Bach ringtone, and everyone froze.

'Yes, Teddy here.' He mouthed 'London' to us.

We all stared with deep concentration.

'What? Where? Why? Sorry, that's a lot to answer. But can you say it again, please?'

He grabbed for a pen and notepaper, jotting something down from instructions on the phone.

'Right, thanks. We'd better get the local police onto this. We'll let you know. Keep in touch, thanks. Bye.'

He replaced the receiver and looked down, biting his lower lip. After ploughing his fingers through his thick crown of hair, he turned to us.

'I'm sorry, everyone. This all seems very weird.'

'Bloody does,' Jackson Coen's voice was heard to comment. That unleashed a hubbub of questions which was stilled only by Teddy's upraised hand.

'Listen. Keep calm. It seems the van has been tracked to a location near the next town down. You passed it on the way from Rome, just a couple of miles from here. Marino Lazio. The van got there at midday and has been there ever since. Why, I don't know. The drivers' phones have been ringing out or going straight to voicemail. The people at the van's firm thought they'd reached their destination, here, as the map shows they're so close. They suggest we get help from the local cops in finding the van, just in case. They're emailing the map to us right now with the tracking information.'

Fabio disappeared into a short corridor behind the desk. Signs indicated it led to the director's office. He reappeared shortly with an printed A4 sheet which he handed over to Teddy. He gestured Teddy to go with him back into the office. A low hum of worried whispered chatter stopped suddenly when the two reappeared a few minutes later, followed by Janet, the Director.

Teddy announced in clear tones, his confidence attempting to reassure us: 'We've spoken to the local Municipal Police, and they're going to meet us in Marino. The van is somewhere there. Fabio and I are taking Janet's car from here, and we'll be there in a matter of minutes. We'll have this cleared up in no time, so go and relax, everyone, and come back here in, say, an hour. I'm sure we'll have your instruments safely here by then. See you later.'

With that, he, Fabio, and an anxious-looking Janet made a path through our group and left through the outside door.

People drifted away, some in small groups, others alone.

'All my sound equipment is in that van. Costs a fortune. I'll kill anyone who messes with it'. The blond technician was clearly in fighting mood.

'That's nothing compared to our instruments,' grumbled Jackson loudly. 'Some of them, mine for one, cost bloody thousands. Six figures! It's irreplaceable.' He flounced off into the garden, red-faced with fury.

I joined some people making themselves tea and coffee in the Internet café, a room with computer screens, kitchenette and coffee tables.

'What do you reckon has happened?' asked Tina, the music librarian, as she and Jeremy invited me to join them over a brew.

Jeremy shrugged and I was no wiser.

'Maybe they broke down,' I offered, obliged to think of something.

'And not telephoned through? Seems unlikely. Unless maybe they went off to find help and left their phones behind.'

'Hm, sounds a bit remote.'

We then changed the subject and talked about the remarkable building and grounds we had pitched up in.

'I believe this used to be a monastery, built over the villa of a Roman consul.'

'Yes, his tomb is outside, on that slab of rock in the top garden, the one the other side of the conference room. You can see outlines of the the bundles of sticks, the fasces, which symbolised his authority, carved in the stone.'

'Where all those funny caves are?'

'Caves?' asked Jeremy who had obviously not explored the series of gardens running alongside the drive and at a higher level than it.

'Yes,' I answered confidently – having discovered these features just a short time earlier. 'And you can see right inside them, carved way back into the rock, arches and ceiling spaces of what look like crypts, but they're mostly silted up with soil, and even rubbish. Such a shame. They'd be fully excavated in England but here Ancient Roman ruins are probably two a penny.'

Tina and I offered to take Jeremy there, and picked up a few more people on the way. We passed along the narrow alley I had discovered earlier and Tina led us across the courtyard where I had heard shouting from one of the bedrooms on the left-hand wall. I accompanied the small party up the steps, through the entrance hall and out into the 'upper gardens', leading them eagerly to my discoveries of caves and their internal chambers.

Afterwards I left that party and joined others lounging on the terrace, taking in the afternoon sun and sipping drinks from the bar. I sat alone at a table with a bottle of Peroni beer and a glass.

'Mind if I join you?'

It was Frank, the oboist. I waved his heavy frame into the chair across from me, as I was just taking a swig. I had not spoken two words with Frank since we started out, although he seemed an amiable sort.

'Isn't this great? The view, the trees, all of this.' He looked around in appreciation.

'It certainly is. Wish we had time to swim – I see they have a pool here.'

'I'd like to come back some other time. Explore these woods a little. Have you been to Italy before?'

I confessed my limited knowledge of the country and asked him the same.

'Yes, we used to live here. In fact Robinson and I both played for the San Carlo opera company in Naples for a couple of seasons. I went up to Venice and played with the Fenice, until the fire. So we went back to London, until that business with Jackson. Then I came out again with Jeffrey Tate.'

I looked none the wiser.

'You know, that conductor with spina bifida. Nice chap.

Got made a CBE and knight and all that. He took over the San Carlo in 2005 and invited me to join him, which I did, until he died five years later. Came home then. Not the same without Mimi, of course.'

'Is that the "we" you mentioned?'

'Yes, happily married, so I thought. She was – is – a costume designer. Still works on commission, I believe, for the odd company. Left me for Jackson, the bastard.'

I left him to glower into his beer glass. I knew how he felt, or at least I imagined I did. I tried to put myself into a man's shoes and wondered if it was any different for them than for us women when we are betrayed. Or is all bretrayal the same? Does it affect everyone the same way? A few words of a poem I had read somewhere came to me:

'Crushed like ice
Like twenty tons have been thrown on my soul ...
So delicately
you devised your plan to kill everything inside me ...'

I wondered if there were as many betrayal poems as there are love ones. As many betrayals as loves. And our reaction to betrayal. Is it always the same? Does everyone go through the same stages as counsellors tell us we do with bereavement? It is a form of the same. A form of death. Worse, in some ways because it colours all of the past.

At least with a loved one's death, the past can be looked back upon with a smile. But when betrayed, the question is always, when did it first happen – not the act, but the preparation for the act, the loss of love? Is all the past a lie, every moment of joy a historic pretence of pleasure? Or did it slowly curdle, until the last moment, the act of treachery?

We both sighed, then he resumed, with more sadness than anger, 'If I were a violent man, I could kill him. But not her. I couldn't harm her, even now.'

Pippa appeared at the doorway and summoned us inside.

'Can you go to the refectory please, and ask anyone else you see to do the same. We're having a meeting. Teddy's back from Marino.'

Teddy and Pippa stood near the refectory door, ushering us in and to be seated. When it seemed that all were assembled, Teddy began.

'Listen everyone. I have some rather alarming news for you – but assure you that the police are on it. We were there when the police found the drivers, John and Riccardo. They were tied up to a tree in the middle of undergrowth near where they say the van was taken. Their mobile phones were put deliberately out of reach and they were pretty pissed off, as you can imagine.'

A great gasp and shouts of 'Oh no!' rang around the refectory.

'Please, let me go on. There was a note pinned on one of them and a large tote bag nearby. It said in Italian ... hang on.' He took out a piece of paper and read the words written on it, 'This is a rough translation:

"If you want your cargo back, safe and sound, fill this bag with half a million euros in twenty euro notes, and leave it at precisely ten a.m. tomorrow on the spot where these men are. If there is anyone with you, or any police involvement whatsoever, your instruments will be smashed and burnt."

A dramatic gasp escaped from just about everyone, and a

loud 'Bugger!' from Jackson.

Teddy looked up and made comforting patting gestures with his hand. He continued, 'The police have the original note and the bag. They'll be running them through tests. They've taken the drivers to interview them and will check their clothing for DNA evidence. There's a unit coming out from Rome to track the van. It seems they disabled the tracking device on it. They knew what they were doing. But the police have their methods. They're bringing in highly trained marksmen should violence be necessary. Let's hope to God it won't be.'

'How are they, John and Riccardo?' a woman's voice calls out.

'Oh, they're fine. A bit shaken, obviously. They'll be seen by medics before being questioned. Fabio has also gone in to help them. Don't forget Riccardo, one of the drivers, is his cousin. Well, ladies and gentlemen, what a day! This is dreadful, I know, but the police are pretty confident the instruments will be found safe.'

'Good God, Italian police – are you kidding?'

'Shut up, Jackson. This is bad enough without you ...'

Several voices called out to silence him. I looked around, choked with concern for these new friends in this time of nightmarish uncertainty. While we were chatting despondently, Teddy received a call on his mobile. After a few moments, he clapped to attract our attention.

'Listen, everyone. Please. I've had Giuseppe, our organiser, Fabio's brother, on the phone from Naples. He's dealing with the police from there. He insists on apologising on behalf of his company for this trouble – says it has never happened before. He says he got the whole story from Fabio and the matter is now in the hands of the State Police, and if necessary, the anti-Mafia branch will be brought in – although it may not come to that.'

There was another audible gasp and eyebrows were raised, 'Mafia!' It could not get worse.

Teddy spoke out again, 'OK! Relax everyone. Peppe says that this sort of thing happens all the time in southern Italy, and only rarely do the police fail to catch the criminals. Modern policing is so effective, its technology is ahead of that of the bad guys.'

That sounded like false reassurance to us, and did little to lighten the mood around the table. Cosima appeared from the kitchen and spoke to Teddy, who then addressed us again,

'Everyone – if you'd like to assemble on the terrace, there'll be some Prosecco or beer for everyone who'd like some – on the house. To help with the wait.'

That evening, after the meal, a disconsolate and anxious group of us went into the lounge, the Hinsley Room, to watch the news on television. Nothing was mentioned about the hijacking of our van. Probably a deliberate news blackout by the police while they are investigating. I sat on the sofa alongside Jackson's desk partner, the bushy-bearded Edward. He spoke mainly to the person on the other side to him, and there were hushed conversations around the room as players swapped vexatious accounts of insurance companies not paying up, and that led on to airline companies sometimes not allowing valuable string instruments to be brought into the cabin but insisting they were stored in the hold. Each account furthered the mood of general misery. I felt something of an outsider, not being a musician, but relieved that I was not in fear of losing something utterly precious, both professional and personal. I just listened quietly to the voices around me.

Then Fabio burst into the room and was instantly the focus of attention.

'Madonna! This day is the worst of my life! Peppe has, what you say "chewed me up". It is not my fault! He tell me to be more vigilant, but what can I do? I cannot travel in the van with the instruments!'

Edward stood up and invited him to be seated on the deep leather sofa, while he perched on the arm. Fabio plonked himself down, the picture of misery. He was such a prima donna.

'What happened? What did the police say?'

'Oh, my poor cousin Riccardo. He and John, the other driver, they are tricked. Another vehicle tell them stop, their back wheel or something is problem. So they pull into a smaller road and stop. They get out, and men from the other car, they come with guns. They tie up our men, my cousin and John, and take the van. They are very scared, Riccardo and John, but is good. They are alive. If Mafia, they are dead. Boom.' He put two fingers up to his forehead mimicking a gun. With this, the room fell silent.

One person spoke up: 'What then, Fabio? Where are the drivers now?'

'They are still with the police. Many questions. I said all I knew and they let me go. But then Peppe, Giuseppe, talk on the telephone and he sends me to hell. I am afraid of him. My own brother!'

There was a murmur of remarks intended to comfort the man, but one after another the occupants left the room, possibly finding the atmosphere just too depressing.

Why did I stay?

Do you really need me to tell you?

Fabio looked at me with those shining intelligent eyes of his, with their almost black pupils, encircled by enviably long and thick lashes. They were welling up with tears. Something inside my midriff fluttered, I could feel my cheeks heating, and suddenly all I wanted to do, more than anything, was to comfort him. My arms ached to encircle him.

'Julia,' he said softly, 'I cannot go to my room. If Giuseppe call me again, I die, I swear. You help me, please Julia.'

We both stood up at the same moment and held each other closely, heads on shoulders.

Then, gently, we unpeeled from each other and he took my hand, guiding me out of the room. From there we walked still hand in hand along to the stairs, up them and down the corridor to my room. We kissed goodbye and I turned and went into the bathroom to take off my mascara and clean my teeth.

On returning, the fully-dressed figure of the most handsome man in all my acquaintance was deeply asleep on my bed. He had taken off his shoes and watch, and that is all. I decided against undressing too, and lay down beside him, trying not to fall off the edge of the narrow bed. He moved over to the wall, unconsciously making room for me. I was too excited, too mentally agitated, to sleep for what seemed like hours. While he was still asleep, he turned and his arm fell over me, pulling me towards him.

As day broke I woke alone. My conscience was clear. Nothing had happened.

This time.

CHAPTER 13

I THREW OPEN THE CURTAINS and shutters to luxuriate in the view – silver glints on the navy-blue lake; sunlight picking out the white buildings on the distant rim on the far side; an azure, pink-tinged sky uncluttered with clouds; clear distant sight of Rome and of the sea. Quickly showering and changing my clothes into fresh ones I almost ran all the way to the outside in order to take a pre-breakfast stroll in the formal gardens adjoining the terrace. When there, I met Freda doing the same.

'Say, I missed all this last night. We got in too late. What a view!'

'How was Venice?'

'Terrific, as ever. But a bit overcrowded, even now. I just wish Americans would stay away!'

We laughed.

'Hey, still no instruments. What a bummer,' she said, her fingers pulling down the ends of her lips replicating a sad face from the emoticons. 'Let's go for a walk this morning – over to the next town through the woods: Nemi. You up for it?'

Why not?

We met up after breakfast at the reception desk where a patient Cosima explained the route with the aid of a photo-copied sketch map of the woods. Freda had kitted herself up as for an expedition in the Andes – walking boots, backpack, forage hat, and a sweater tied around her waist.

'I always go for a hike wherever I am,' she explained, 'so I come prepared. Hence the big heavy suitcase!'

All I had put on differently were shoes and socks instead of sandals. We studied the map, noting a few landmarks, such as 'fallen tree', 'dried river bed', 'underpass', 'ancient Roman paving'. If we followed the right path we could reach Nemi in a couple of hours.

'It's a town worth going to,' encouraged Cosima. 'It is famous for wild strawberries – you can get a lovely pastry with your coffee. Nemi means "Sacred Grove" and Diana was worshipped there.'

'How exciting!' Freda beamed.

'And if you are very tired, you can call for a taxi. Here's the number. You can walk back on the road, but it is very dangerous – nowhere to walk, only fast traffic. Good luck. Also, this is the code for the gate, coming back.'

We set out through the formal garden towards the end where a gateway and spiral staircase were carved out of the solid cliff-face. We entered the dark and narrow entrance, climbed the stone steps and passed through an iron gate secured by a numberpad lock.

We emerged onto an uphill slope beyond the precinct of the villa, alongside land belonging to a hotel perched on the clifftop above the villa. We passed the hotel's tennis courts and came to a meadow which we crossed diagonally, heading for a line of trees. Finding a gap in the length of wire-net fencing, Freda and I stepped through it and entered into a dense woodland with many possible tracks in all directions.

Trees, bushes and thickets of undergrowth grew in free and natural profusion. We scanned the sketched map and decided on a route – basically heading north east, according to the position of the sun. As we walked we could recognise some indicators on the map – a fallen tree trunk, a dead tree stump, a red mark painted on bark. But, hold on, there's a trunk over there too and a couple of dead stumps in this direction!

Some paths became clear, others were obscured by thick brambles and low branches. A riverbed was treacherous, with loose stones filling the v-shaped trough. But we managed to negotiate some of its length and walked on, feeling like explorers in an undiscovered land, until we hit a wider well-trodden path. A group of cyclists filed past us on mountain bikes, returning Freda's '*Ciao!*' and '*Buon Giorno!*'

We found the road underpass with its pebbly path, and emerging into even deeper woodland. When we could walk abreast, we laughed and joked, Freda feeding little bits of comic information about the day in Venice she had spent with her coterie of young musicians.

'Say, guess what I learned yesterday about that Jackson creep?' she said, turning serious. I looked interested.

'Y'know Wing, that great young violinist? He's got a sister, Maili – don't ya love their names? They all mean something. Hers means "beautiful", isn't that neat! — anyway, she is a fantastic pianist, apparently, although she's only seventeen.

Wants to come to London to study where her brother does, but that bastard Jackson won't sign the papers to get her a visa. He's stopped the others doing so too as he's in charge of the admissions team, or something. Laughed in Wing's face when he went to appeal the decision. Told him to go home if he didn't like it. What an SOB.'

I paused for a moment to take it all in and to work out what the initials stood for, then registered my genuine feelings.

'Bastard!'

Just as we were feeling a little tired, we found a path almost clear of soil and leaves, with ancient Roman paving flags. Trudging along it, my imagination played with pretending to be a citizen of Ancient Rome making a pilgrimage to Diana's shrine. Then, through the foliage, another, smaller, lake came into view, its waters sparkling and twinkling. Buoyed by the appearance of our journey's end we found new energy and shortly found ourselves walking through the portal into the ancient walled town of Nemi.

'This is great,' said Freda, wiping pastry crumbs from around her mouth. 'Best strawberry tartlet ever! I'm not so tired now, how about we walk back? Just a sec. I'll see if the van's turned up yet.' She made a call on her mobile and shook her head. 'No, not yet. But the police are onto something and Teddy says there should be a breakthrough soon. I guess we've time to walk back – and I so love these woods.'

I felt rested after a coffee and strawberry ice-cream, sitting at a table overloooking Lake Nemi with its historic connections. A smaller than life-sized bust of the Emperor Caligula was attached to a wall nearby, as if the citizens were not too sure about acknowledging him or not. I had read that this was the lake on which he floated massive luxury barges, conducting some of his notorious orgies.

'Let's go!' Freda led and I followed, happily allowing her to work out how to retrace our route. When with a stronger personality than mine, I am happy to be a passenger. Otherwise, I tend to do the leading. With David, we took it in turns. Back along the ancient path Freda and I went, through the underpass, taking this path and that – occasionally retracing our steps to undo a wrong turn. We acknowledged, with cries of glee, markers recently passed on our outward journey.

After some time, feeling we may have followed a wrong direction we decided on a short break to gulp down some water in the plastic bottles with us and to study the map. We could hear traffic on a road nearby and knew we did not want to be any nearer to it. We headed for what we saw was a break in the trees, a little oasis dappled with sunlight surrounded by dense undergrowth.

As we entered the sunlit open space I could hear voices alternately raised in anger, then sinking to quieter whispers. They came from men standing on the far side of a screen of trees and undergrowth on the outer edge of our clearing. Freda, smiling, put her finger to her lips and, just for fun, tiptoed over to the thicket from behind which came the voices. She moved very slowly and quietly, to eavesdrop on the conversation. I peered between the leaves of a low tree, holding a thin branch back to take a look.

Three men were engaged in an altercation in Italian, one facing me, one with his back towards me, and one hidden from my view. The one facing me was of middle age and scruffily dressed, with a deep, rasping voice. The one with his back to me was younger, taller and wearing a leather jacket and a baseball cap. His voice was higher pitched, a tenor's. They were arguing with the third man, out of my sight, and whose voice sounded strong, clearer and pitched at a tone between the other two. Had I heard it before? Surely not.

I noticed the roadway passed behind where the men were standing and two motorcycles were parked on the verge. The occasional lorry passed by, drowning out the voices. Suddenly Freda made a slight gasp which drew my attention to her. Her eyebrows had shot up her forehead with alarm, and she repeated the finger-to-lip command for silence. I remained rooted, suddenly afraid, and concentrated on listening to the words the men were saying, but could make no sense of them. I wished I had learnt Italian. Freda had, and as noiselessly as possible in walking boots, crept towards me, still signing for silence.

When I could almost feel her breath on my face, she whispered urgently, 'They're talking about the instruments and the van. They must be involved. Quick, let's get outta here. Don't make a sound. Back to the villa, come on.'

I shivered as a chill passed through me, followed by an adrenaline rush of excitement as Freda, amazingly light-footed, passed me and gestured to follow her. I lost no time and we both hurriedly left the clearing. From the voices I heard a commanding, 'Zitto!' and then an abrupt silence.

'Oh God, they've heard us. Come on!' Freda mouthed, and waved for me to hurry even more quickly towards her. By now my heart was fairly bursting out of the ribcage. I had been in danger before, but this was different. We were running from people – possibly mafiosi, who spent their lives mired in blackmail, abduction, and murder.

We plunged back into the dense undergrowth, threading

along what passed for a path until we reached the dried watercourse tumbled with rocks of all sizes. We heard breaking twigs and what could have been heavy footsteps behind us, but when I turned to look, could see nobody there. There was so much cover provided by trees and bushes, though, that followers could easily hide themselves. Or perhaps they had taken a different route and would cut us off further along? My legs started to feel like jelly, the fear beginning to affect me.

'Come on, Julia,' I urged myself, 'this is not the time to give up or go slowly. Move your butt, girl!'

I looked up at Freda ahead and seemingly unperturbed, with an expression of quiet determination. From time to time she waved, encouraging me to keep up. With sufficient caution we negotiated the loose stones littering the narrow gorge, climbing upwards as speedily as possible.

'If I fell here,' I thought, 'I'd break an ankle, at least. Then what?'

We made it without incident out onto flat and firm ground again, and I was relieved to recognise some further features of our onward journey: the fallen tree, the red painted sign on a tree trunk, the dead stump, the path that split into several directions.

After our hurried start, we eased off the pace as we detected no sound or other sign of being followed. We allowed ourselves short pauses to gasp and pant and to slug water from our bottles. We even began to make jokes about the situation. Freda is definitely the person to have beside you in a crisis. She turns everything into fun. Her stamina far exceeded mine and I realised that she was not nearly as out of breath as I was. Singing training, probably.

It was when we were not far from the edge of the woods and close to the meadow beyond that disaster struck.

'Bloody hell!'

A thin root, anchored at both ends in the parched clay, served as a tripwire and my right foot caught under it. I thumped my left foot down to save me from falling, but at an unnatural angle. A intense, sharp pain seared through it. I instantly lost balance, falling heavily to the ground where I crunched my elbow on the stoney ground.

'Ow! God, it hurts!' I could not help crying out loud.

Freda returned to me, all commiseration and concern. Our eyes immediately scoured the route we had just taken for any sign of pursuers. There was none. We breathed more deeply, but both my foot and elbow began to throb with excruciating pain.

'You poor thing. Can you walk?'

I tried to stand, but sank down again with several 'Ows!'

'Hey, that's too bad. You just stay there, don't move, I'll think of something. Did you bring the number of the Villa? No, neither did I. I'll try Teddy.'

She drew out her phone and pressed a key. She peered at it closely.

'Damn, there's no signal here. Must be the only dead spot in Italy. Stay tight and I'll run and get some help. We're almost there now – it won't take long. Cry out if there's any trouble, but there really shouldn't be any.'

She paused, possibly wondering about the wisdom of what she said next, 'You couldn't understand what those guys were saying, so they'll not come after you. Why should they? You didn't see any of them, did you? And I may have got mixed up anyway and it could all be perfectly innocent. Just a few guys arguing in a wood ... Won't be long. OK?'

I assured her I'd be fine – sitting there in the shade of trees, nursing my throbbing elbow and cursing my stupid ankle. She left and all seemed quiet. An occasional bird sang nearby and a lizard darted away nearby. Some ants crawled over my leg.

What was that?

A rustle in the undergrowth.

People? Birds?

Then I remembered Cosima saying that there were wild boar in the woods. I sat more still than before, considering what the sensible response should be to being discovered by a boar.

But it was not a wild boar that smashed a weight on my head. A moment's agonising pain, then the lights went out.

CHAPTER 14

I CAME TO, groggy of thought and misty of vision. I smelt close-up to my nose the primordial scent of sun-baked leaves and earth. Bracken and tiny twigs were scratching my face. My left elbow throbbed, and so did the back of my head.

I was judderingly aware that I could not breathe through my mouth. Something was gagging me, making me retch, some fabric. This shouldn't be there, whatever it is. I panicked, heart throbbing painfully. My fingers drew out the obstruction. It was a sock. I squinted at it against the light. One of mine. How the hell? I wriggled the toes of first my right foot, then the left. Yes, my right foot was bare, and as I felt my toes moving, I thanked God my left foot was not broken, just painful.

Voices approached. The incoherent vocal sounds gave way to a jumble of words,

'Oh my God, Julia! '

'What the hell happened to you?'

'Stay still, don't move.'

'Who did this?'

'How are you?'

I pushed myself up on my right elbow and faces took form as I looked up: Freda's, Jackson's, Philip Robinson's. They were inches from my own, drowning me in concern and relief.

Just then the back of my head crashed with agony. The pain –moderate throbbing before – now really connected. Jagged lights shot through my eyes, then all sight was blurred. I felt suddenly sick. I swayed, about to vomit. Nothing came beyond my throat, but I began to shiver uncontrollably and saliva filled my mouth. Hands gently gripped under my arms, while someone put on my right shoe, minus the sock. I was helped up to my knees, and then, only briefly, onto my feet.

'Ooow!' I am no Stoic.

The moment my left foot touched the ground the sharp intense pain in it forced me to stumble forwards. Fortunately Jackson's arms were there to stop my fall.

'Lean on me' he offered, and his and Robinson's arms made a cradle for my back. I tried hopping, but progress was slow. The two men, as one, then took all of my weight and carried me between them.

The thinking part of my head was floating airily, the approaching hotel seemed to draw fuzzily closer then withdraw, the sunlight dimmed then brightened, and sounds swirled incoherently. The back part of my skull was anything but light. It felt as if it were exploding, as if it was being crashed into every few moments.

It was not the first time I had been bashed on the head – it should have had callouses by now. I raised a hand to feel what must have been a bump, but brought it away with blood on it.

'Seems you were hit with a log,' said Jackson when he and my other porter paused for breath. 'There's bits of bark in your hair. I wouldn't touch it again if I were you. Get it seen to first.'

While he and Robinson carried me out of the woods and across the field, I could hear Freda talking about something that was on the ground near where I had been. She mentioned taking photographs on her mobile and said she'd show them to me when we got back.

We made our way back past the hotel and down the rock staircase with heroic effort. I was released from the cradle of arms and simply supported by them as I hopped down each step on one foot. When our little party emerged into the garden, a number of people, I cannot recall just who, rushed forwards towards us to help me, taking my weight off Jackson and Robinson.

They fussed generally until we made it to the Internet café room. Liz was there in conference with her technicians. They broke off when we arrived and she made me a mug of tea while Freda went off muttering, 'I must find Teddy.'

Jackson meanwhile took charge, shooing people out of the room.

'Give her some space, now. Come on.'

Robinson passed me the tea from Liz. Jackson gave a tug on Robinson's shirt sleeve,

'Hey, Florence Nightingale, can you go and get Janet and the police? Freda's gone for Teddy. There're still some cops around. Go and do something useful.'

Robinson left on his mission, and I found a few moments peace. I tried to stop my head from swirling, and felt Jackson placing a gentle hand on my forehead, as if he understood the need to quieten the turbulence. It seemed to help. I looked at him gratefully. He was without his usual bluster and arrogance so, since my head had cleared, I dared to ask,

'Why do you tease Philip Robinson? You seem to be close but you treat him like a naughty child. He's really very nice.'

'Oh, don't worry about it. We've always been like that. It's a bit of an act. I'm really quite fond of the bugger. But I can't help teasing him. He seems to draw it out of me, being weak I suppose. Just takes it.'

He sat down beside me and spoke in an even more confidential manner, quite seriously,

'And I don't know whether or not to tell him about his daughter and her resit exam. I had to fail her again. She's really just not up to it. It's a tough profession, and it's no good being second best. As I said to you before, I'd sooner leave it to her to break it to him, but I'll probably just blurt it out over a drink, and that'll be me being bad old Jackson again.'

'Oh, I'm sorry. I didn't mean to ...'

Just then, Janet arrived, followed by Freda and two uniformed policemen. Jackson went to join Robinson standing, hovering behind them, listening but not interfering.

'Hi, Julia. I'm really sorry to hear you've been attacked. That's never happened before here. But we'll get you to a hospital to sort you out.'

She turned to the police and spoke to them in Italian, then to Freda and me. One of the police left quickly.

'I've told them that this lady is going to the San Giuseppe hospital in Albano first, then they can question her all they like. I'll take you myself.'

She turned back to the policeman and issued further instructions. The other returned pushing a wheelchair which both he and Janet helped me into. I was taken along the cloister, down a wooden ramp in the entrance porch and then out into the expanded area at the end of the drive where a few cars were parked. Janet opened the passenger door of the first car and I was lowered gently into it.

A few minutes later, my head, ankle and elbow were being examined by a young woman in a white coat. She was a wild-haired, black-eyed beauty, somewhat averse to smiling. She asked a few questions in excellent English and noted my squawks of pain when she put finger pressure onto certain points on my skull, arm and foot. I had all my aching, throbbing injuries x-rayed. Then I sat and waited in a corridor.

After some time, which I spent feeling sorry for myself, I was called in to see the stern-faced young doctor. She showed me the x-rays of my foot, arm and head. Nothing broken, thank God. My ankle was bound with a compression wrap, my elbow bandaged, and a patch of hair at the back of my head shaved to enable application of an enormous dressing.

After this reassuring interview with the doctor, an older stout and very short woman took me to a ward where she helped me to undress down to my bra and pants, and tucked me into a bed in a room with three other occupied beds. Under the silent scrutiny of the other patients, and although it was only late afternoon, I soon fell into a drug-induced sleep and stayed unconscious until the next morning.

CHAPTER 15

THE NEXT MORNING I was effectively wakened by the shot of caffeine brought to me with what passes for breakfast in Italy, a croissant with jam and a piece of sponge cake. Still, having it in bed was something of a treat — reminding me painfully of the times, rare but precious, when David would waken me with a tray of cereal, toast and marmalade and a small pot of tea.

With help from another tiny nurse, half my size and seemingly half my age, I was dressed and sent on to a physiotherapist. The massage she gave my sprained left foot and ankle was a contrasting mixture of pain and soothing.

Brisk and efficient, this skilled practitioner possessed minimal English but I managed to follow what she said about movement exercises, and took from her a paper with photographs of lower legs and accompanying instructions in Italian but which even I could understand. She also provided me with a pair of crutches: grey aluminium sticks with plastic braces to circle my upper arms, and sturdy grips to hold. She demonstrated how to use them, and we giggled at my first wobbly efforts.

The same kindly young nurse who had helped me to dress then reappeared and guided me to the reception, where I signed some papers – whatever they were. After fishing in my shoulder bag, I found my European health insurance card and debit card and gave them to the grave-faced man who had asked for them, signed some more papers, and sat in the waiting area.

Just before nine o'clock, Freda herself came to collect me by taxi.

'Honey! You poor thing, how are you?'

'Honestly, I'm fine, thanks. No need for any fuss, my head is solid – the benefit of thick bones, and my ankle is not broken, just badly sprained. I'll be ...'

My protestations were cut short by the excitement of my friend.

'That's good. Now, hey, great news! The instruments are back – all safe and sound!'

'Crime solved? Criminals arrested?'

'Hold on! One thing at a time!'

'Tell me what happened. Did they get whoever clobbered me?'

Freda seemed suddenly subdued, 'Not exactly.' She looked away, 'I should be in rehearsal right now ...' That was lame, and I felt disappointed. I thought she would be straight with me.

'Oh never mind that! Please tell me what happened.'

'OK, when you're home. It's a long story.'

When we pulled up, Janet was waiting with the wheelchair.

'Would you like another room – one on the ground floor?'

'No, thanks. I'd sooner stay where I am. The view is spectacular, these crutches are great, and the stairlift should help me get up and down.'

Between Freda and Janet, and all the appliances for mobility, I made it to my room and sat reclined on the bed with pillows propping me up. Janet left, and Freda drew up the chair from under the desk.

'Well, honey. After you left for the hospital yesterday, the cops searched the woods, but could not come up with anything. Say, it was good they were in the house here dealing with the stuff about the van, as they shot to the scene real quick.'

'And, did they find anything?'

'They did find the wood log that those bastards hit you with – it had bloodstains on it. They took it away for examination. There was also something else, right by where you were lying. This ...'

She pulled out her mobile and showed me a photograph. At first I could not see what I was supposed to be looking at.

'See? The sticks – the 'T' shape they're making on the ground? Get it?'

'No. I can see them, but haven't a clue what they mean.'

'Well, it means the same as the sock they put in your mouth. Oh, the cops have taken that too. And your hairbrush for DNA. Listen honey, don't get scared ... but these are Mafia signs.'

Don't get scared? I began to tremble.

'Stuffing your mouth means "Don't say anything" – sometimes found on the bodies of guys who split on them. And the

T stands for *"Tacere, oppure"*, that means – be quiet, or else. Nice, huh?'

My trembling became visible, even to Freda who had been too excited with her news to notice the effect it was having on me.

She frowned, and took my hand, 'Hey, don't worry about it. You're here. Safe.'

I tried to talk normally, but a funny growling voice came out of me, 'So the Mafia are after me to see that I don't talk? Great! About what? I couldn't understand a word they said. But ...'

I felt a sudden jolt in my stomach and must have reflected the feeling in a horrified look.

'What, Julia?'

'I did see one of them, fully.'

She drew a sharp intake of breath. 'Oh, really?'

'I only saw the second one's back and I didn't see the third man, but I think I recognised his voice.'

'Who? You don't know anyone here!'

'No, but it could have been Fabio's.'

She gasped, 'No!'

I did something then that I have no doubt everybody does when they have had more than they can cope with – I cried. Sobs and tears. Gasps and sobs. Howls even, and lots of tears. Freda's arms encircled me and I could hear her soothing words, though I knew I had to cry all my fears and pain until I was done. I cried myself into unconsciousness.

When I came to, Teddy and Pippa were sitting at my bedside on chairs. Father Hayes was standing near the door. Freda, perched on the bed, was holding my hand. The eyes of all of them expressed tender concern. It felt strangely pleasant being the object of such empathy.

'How are you feeling now?' Teddy asked sympathetically.

'Uh, OK, I s'ppose,' I muttered incoherently.

'If you need me at all,' said the clergyman, 'just tip me the wink. I'll be praying for you. I'll leave you with your friends now, but I'll be back if there's anything I can do – sacrament of the sick, or anything.'

I smiled my thanks and, after nodding his farewell, he left.

'What's happened?' I croaked.

Teddy answered, 'Well, the main thing is, you're with us – safe and well, or going to be. Of course you're upset – who wouldn't be. I think Freda is rather taking the Mafia thing a bit literally. The police tell us that plenty of small-time crooks use the Mafia as cover to scare off witnesses and so on. In this area it's the *Camorra*, the Neapolitan outfit, and while they have traditionally been involved in street crime – robbery and suchlike, these days they are into much bigger pickings than nicking a few musical instruments. Their projects now involve corrupting politicians and obtaining all the large-scale building contracts.'

He stopped and the rest of us nodded as though we knew all about the underground world of crime and extortion.

He continued, 'Fabio was telling me that if the real Mafia, the Camorra, find people taking their name in vain, abusing their reputation, they can punish them rather more harshly than the justice system does. So if anything, the *capos* of the Camorra are rather on *our* side in this case than against us. Good thing, eh? The police think so too. So don't give it a thought. Anyway, you're perfectly safe here and will not be on your own at all.'

'You've got the instruments back?'

'Yes, that's the good news.'

Both Teddy and Pippa looked relieved to be able to talk about something positive. They took it in turns to tell the tale, leaning forward when their turn came.

'Well', began Pippa, 'you probably heard how our drivers, were jumped on when they stopped to check the van.'

Teddy took over, 'You couldn't see the place from the road, it was in a little copse of scrub and bushes. They threw their mobiles phones there, just out of reach!'

Pippa leant forward, 'Apparently, then the car chaps drove off with the van, leaving a blackmail note where we'd find it – and a bag to put the loot. Poor John and Riccardo are feeling very guilty, as if they're responsible for the theft – but there's nothing they could have done. The robbers had guns!'

'How did they find the van if the tracking device had been disabled, which you assumed must have happened?' Freda asked.

'Fortunately,' Pippa's eyes shone as she relayed this, 'an off-duty policeman was going home for lunch when he noticed the van with English wording on it and an GB numberplate, and men acting suspiciously around it. They seemed to have scarves over their faces, you know, those Palestinian chequered ones with fringes and tassels. He just knew something wasn't as it should be.'

'Coppers' instinct, David would say,' I added involuntarily. Why mention David?

'Thank goodness for it! Anyhow, he hid his vehicle a little further along, walked back and noted the number plate of an old banger on the side of the road, the ones the men were using, and then turned for home, intending to call it in sometime. While he went back to work after his long lunch-break, he heard the alert put out by one or other of the police forces – there seem to be dozens of different ones round here – about the vanjacking. He knew he had seen it happen earlier.'

'Wow, good for him!'

She continued, almost breathless with the fun of it all.

'It turns out the number plates on the car were from a vehicle owned by a crash victim in the Naples area who died a couple of years ago and whose vehicle had been a write-off.'

'Stolen number plates!'

'Anyway, there's a farm not far from Marino which had recently been bought by a character from Naples with a police record.'

'The police had been keeping tabs on him,' added Teddy.

'Yes, so yesterday morning the cops followed some suspects from the farm to the collection point ...'

'Where they lifted the bag the police had filled with fake Euros,' Teddy explained.

'And back to the farm. When they got there, armed police raided the farm and found the van with everything still in it – all the instruments, sound equipment, stands and everything! It was in a shed, keeping cool, thank God. The van's temperature controls weren't on, but the shed was cool.'

'That was so lucky. They could all have been ruined, left in the sun. Jackson's Amati violin alone would have been almost worthless if exposed to the heat or if they'd taken it out and tossed it around. That is the most valuable all of the instruments, by a long way. But they all have value to their owners, of course.'

'Doesn't bear thinking about!'

'Absolutely. The police took the van in for forensics and

brought it back early this morning. I've been rehearsing all morning and everybody is just so happy to have their precious instruments back.'

'And the robbers?'

Teddy frowned.

'Er, no. Not yet. There was a bit of a shoot-out at the farm and one of the guys got shot – no, the police are fine. It's thought the old man was giving covering fire while the others escaped at the back. A couple of motorbikes roared off and the police lost them.'

'The men in the woods!' Freda exclaimed. There was silence while we took in the implications of that.

I then had another troubling idea.

'How did they know that the van contained expensive instruments such as Jackson's violin?'

Teddy and Pippa looked at each other, while Freda stood up to look out of the window.

'We don't know,' said Teddy. 'It could simply be the name of the van company "Harmony Transport", decorated with pictures of musical notes and instruments. Or someone, perhaps in Padua or even Milan, could have tipped them off.'

He frowned and lowered his voice, 'Or, and this doesn't bear thinking about, it could have been an inside job. Someone here told them where the van would be and when.'

All went silent. A chill seemed to pass through the room. Freda turned from studying the view out of the window, determined to be optimistic.

'I'm sure that's out of the question,' she said with a rather forced jollity. Nobody in our party, or Liz's, or Fabio's, would do such a thing. No it must have been one of those porters in

Padua who helped unload and load up again. The cops will find them, don't worry.'

We could hear orchestral playing coming from the conference room not far beyond my bedroom.

'Uh-uh, I'd better go,' announced Teddy. 'The natives will be getting restless. Frank conducts when I'm not there, but they'll want to pack up soon. It's nearly eleven and we have to finish by half past at the latest,' he said, looking at Pippa. 'Sorry, Julia, must dash. Don't get up until you feel like it, OK?'

After he left, I voiced the concern that had been bothering me. Freda resumed her silent hand-holding.

'So just who were the people in the woods? Why were they there and why clobber me? When will they be caught?'

'I suppose they had just escaped from the farmhouse shooting, and were arguing about who had betrayed them. The police are fairly sure they know who two of them are, just not the third. It seems odd that they should meet up so close to the Villa, unless …' Pippa left the rest unsaid.

'Unless they were meeting someone from our group,' Freda finished for her, slowly twisting her mouth into a grimace of worry. This was not like Freda. She added, thoughtfully, 'After all, we saw only two motorbikes, so the third guy must have walked there.'

Pippa and I lapsed into a thoughtful silence. The only Italians in our group were Fabio and his cousin, Riccardo the driver. The driver was with the police at that time. It couldn't possibly be Fabio. Lots of men have baritone voices similar to his. He's far too gentle to wallop me on the head. Isn't he?

Pippa then spoke with quiet urgency, 'I've got something to say now that you may not like.'

How much more could I take? As if being bashed on the head, possibly by my Latin lover, and threatened by the Mafia with 'or else', were not enough.

'Yesterday, when you went off to hospital, I had a word with Teddy and …'

'Yes?'

'Well, we both thought it best. We rang your mother, you know, the next-of-kin number you gave, and she passed us over to your husband.'

'You spoke to David?' I gulped, and the last grain of strength left every cell of my body. Could this be happening?

'Well yes. We thought he should know. Of course he was deeply concerned and …'

Her hesitation told me everything.

'He's coming here?'

'Yes, sorry,' she grimaced. 'Said he'd get the earliest flight he could this morning. Should be here any time.'

CHAPTER 16

I HAD TO REFLECT upon that development, but my head was hurting too much. I could only feel a surge of emotion, an indefinite mixture of anger and embarrassment and sickening disappointment. I had been the strong one, the decision-maker, the one who reacted to betrayal by calmly walking away. Now David would see me as a victim, someone who needed his reassuring presence. How could I have any control of my life if David is sent for as a saviour without whom I cannot survive. No, no!

Silence ensued as Pippa and Freda discreetly left me to my thoughts. Then Pippa stood up.

'Hey, Freda, you and I should practise that duet. There's a grand piano in the television lounge, let's go. It's only a matter of hours before the show.'

'Sure, sorry. Well, Kiddo, I guess you won't be doing your narrating tonight.'

I channelled the anger I was feeling at their interference into a stout denial.

'I certainly shall!' I attempted to get up from the bed. I am not a wimp. I am a survivor, a conqueror over adversity.

'Hey, OK! Gottit! Listen, there's a couple of hours before lunch. Why don't you get a bit of rest and then see how you feel.'

'That's good advice,' added Pippa. 'It'll be great if you feel fit enough to go on tonight. But don't push yourself. See how you are. If that head still hurts, don't do it.'

In the face of their genuine concern and kindness I could not maintain my childish tantrum. I acquiesced, sinking back into the pillows as the two slipped out. I found the confusion of thoughts and feelings really tiring and drifted off to sleep with the sound of music wafting down the corridor.

I came to, suddenly disoriented. My head hurt, my elbow and, yikes, my foot too. There was bright daylight and I was fully clothed. Not dawn, then. I remembered – I had suffered concussion and been discharged from hospital. There was no longer any sound of music. I remembered hearing it before I dozed off and that the rehearsal was due to finish at half past eleven. My watch showed it was long past midday. I must have been out for more than an hour. If I wanted to catch a moment in the sun on the terrace before lunch, I had better get up. I reached for the crutches and gripped the handles and with my upper arms threaded into the cuffs, I hopped into the corridor.

Nelson was hurrying ahead of me, just at the bend in the corridor. He was carrying his double bass in a hard shell case, holding it upright in front of him. I thought I caught a glimpse of another person, just ahead of him, or rather a flash of something bright blue, but could not really see and was preoccupied with keeping my balance. Something was on my mind, and I tried to prise it out. Oh, idiot. That's me. Of course, I would need my posh frock and shoes for the concert. Or shoe, singular. I would not want to come back for them after lunch. Back to the room.

I gathered my performance outfit, script and make-up bag, and put them all into one smart shop-bag. Then made my way out again, carefully clicking shut the door behind me and feeling in my trouser pocket that my key-card was safe.

I limped along and settled into the stairlift, slowly descending the two flights of stone steps. At their foot I hesitated for only a second at the choice of direction. One direction is to take the underpass beneath the chapel, for which there is a note requesting guests to travel this route, particularly when people are using the chapel for prayers and services. The other is to go through the chapel, only allowed for disabled people and when nobody is at prayer inside. Naturally I took the shortcut through the chapel, emerging onto the corridor with the reception desk halfway along it. Cosima was checking in a newcomer, a man with a small suitcase next to him.

David.

I stopped, unsure of my reaction. Was I pleased to see him, or outraged?

I knew my heart rate was racing.

Although the Villa was cool, I felt a sudden rush of heat, so much that perspiration beaded my face and my clothes began to stick to me clammily.

Just after he put down a pen and handed over his passport, he turned his face in my direction.

'Julia!'

He bounded towards me, pulling up sharply as he saw my expression – not the most welcoming.

'I had to come,' he said apologetically. 'I heard what happened to you and, well, I couldn't leave you like that ...'

That voice. His voice. Him, standing right there, not three feet away from me. Hit him? Turn away? Be cool and dismissive?

No. What did I do?

Bursting into tears, I dropped my bag and lunged at him with my arms outstretched, crutches dangling, and hugged him for all I was worth. He held me tight, muttering soothingly,

'Hey, its all right. I'm here now. Shush, shush. All will be well, and all will be well ...'

I joined in with 'And all manner of things will be well.' We laughed. That saying of Julian of Norwich was a mantra of comfort one of us would use to cheer the other. Oh, happy days. Lost forever?

We arrived together in front of a beaming Cosima.

'Perhaps we could have a double room, my wife and I?'

'No' I protested. This is too rushed. 'Please, I'm fine – all settled in. Sorry but it's too soon yet. Let's see how it goes.'

He was embarrassed and disappointed. I did not enjoy hurting him, but decided that reconciliation would take more than a sudden outburst of emotion on my part. It would be a journey, and we had taken only the first step.

Well, second, if his flying out could be considered the first.

David moved his suitcase round beside the reception desk, out of my way as I hobbled towards the terrace. He followed and quite sensibly, went off to the bar to fetch a couple of drinks. When he returned we sat in silence; I was unsure which of us should speak first or about what. Then Freda and Pippa joined us. They can talk to him, I thought. After all, it was their fault he was here at all. I sat back, eyes closed, basking in the sunshine, while Freda entertained the party with jokes and anecdotes. She's a star.

Shortly afterwards we heard the bell for lunch and headed for the refectory. When everyone was seated, Teddy stood up and introduced David to the group, sitting beside me. Vaclav and Wing, opposite, made polite conversation about the weather, his flight and generalities. It was all fairly embarrassing.

At the end of the meal Teddy stood up to make another official announcement, hitting his glass with a spoon to request silence.

'OK, everyone. The van is here, and our new temporary drivers are with it outside. Please could you load up your instruments. The drivers are both Italian and don't speak English, so give yourself a bit more time to explain the packing process. Our own men, John and Riccardo have been taken to Rome to help the police enquiry, but we expect them here for the trip to Naples tomorrow.'

'Is the coach here too?'

'The coach will pick us up outside at three o'clock. So, I see many of you have changed already. You others, don't forget to wear or bring your performance clothes as we shan't be coming back after the final rehearsal down there.'

A few heads turned, looking for someone.

CHAPTER 17

I SAT ON THE COACH next to David. After everyone was seated several minutes passed with nothing happening. It was after three o'clock.

Teddy stood at the front, facing us, handheld microphone poised.

'Has anyone seen Jackson?'

Various murmurs followed, 'Where is the bloody man?'

Someone called out, 'This is too much – drive on Teddy!'

Then Pippa stood beside her husband and took the microphone.

'I went to the conference room a few minutes ago and Jackson's kit is still there. His violin, everything. He was not in his room, either. We'll give him another few minutes. Meanwhile, I'll pop back and tell Cosima to let him know we've gone and that he'll have to take a taxi. Of course, he wasn't here earlier when you said three o'clock. But it's jolly annoying, all the same.'

It was not like Pippa to be negative. 'Jolly annoying' was strong language for her.

We arrived at the Parco della Musica and the group was taken on a tour of the impressive contemporary complex of auditoriums, studios, museums and galleries. I took one look at the plan of the buildings and opted out, on account of my foot.

David and I made for the Spartito restaurant instead, and we sat over a coffee, making awkward conversation.

'How's my mother?'

'She's fine. Ronald's a character though!'

'Really? In what way?' I found that hard to believe.

'The way he dotes on her. Does everything she asks. Seems like a teenager in love. Strange man.'

I barely took in what else we said. It was all fairly bland and inconsequential. His parents were much the same as when I left them, and the poor girl from next door, brain damaged and now orphaned, had settled in well and seemed to be enjoying life.

I was churning with conflicting emotions yet felt very mature sitting there, having this conversation. Highly civilised. Inside, part of me harboured murderous thoughts and yet ... I wanted him so much. I wondered, was I being a prima donna, putting on this hard face, resisting his warmth? Was he capable of truly loving me? While he was loving another, was he comparing us, finding her more ... something – attractive, flirtatious, desirable, attentive, what? Was I to blame? Or do all men need a little 'something on the side'? God, I can talk. What about Fabio?

I think I probably blushed at this moment.

Fortunately, at that point when I came out of my reverie,

David was paying the bill. He did not need to ask about my change of complexion. He helped me maneouvre the crutches and we joined the rest of the group after their tour. We all proceded to the Sala Sinopoli where, eventually, after collecting instruments from somewhere backstage, arranging seating and tuning up, the orchestra rehearsed. I was given a seat on the stage, so only had to hop a few feet to stand and deliver my narrative.

By the evening we were gathered in the Green Room behind the auditorium, finishing sandwiches and bottled water provided by Teddy and Fabio. The soloists had changed into their finery, and everyone else into black, formal clothing. I had on my plum-coloured kaftan that I had worn on previous evenings – and hoped it was not too smelly by now. While the auditoriums were all air-conditioned and cool, nerves caused my temperature to sky-rocket. Freda approached me, all concerned. She had been chatting merrily to David in the Green Room, but now was all seriousness.

'Where the hell is Jackson? He really is the limit, leaving it as late as this.'

Tina, the music librarian, and Philip Robinson were nearby and overheard, joining us with similar worries.

'If he doesn't come soon,' noted Philip, 'we'll either have to drop the Tartini, or someone else will have to play.'

'I know Edward would like to,' Tina said quietly. 'He told me how he was green with envy that Jackson is always lead violin with all the juicy solos. He's just as good a musician ... played in the Berlin with Von Karajan for a season. Knows the Trill perfectly.'

Tina had an in-depth knoweldge about everyone. As a

non-player, she mixed with them all, and her knowledge of the music earned their respect.

Just at that moment, Teddy called for silence.

'Listen, everyone. It seems there's a wee bit of a crisis, as Jackson has not arrived and seems to be nowhere in the Villa. Janet has looked all over for him, and there's no sign. That was a couple of hours ago, and he hasn't turned up yet.'

'Maybe he's lost – gave the taxi driver the wrong address, or something,' suggested Simon.

His friend Jude added: 'Or maybe he went for a walk in the woods and got lost there, thinking he'd have plenty of time to get here.'

Teddy nodded. 'Either are possibilities, although he told me that he had been to this venue before, when on holiday last year. So he should know where we are. Anyway Edward, are you up to playing the Trill? We can announce that Jackson is "indisposed" and you have stepped in at the last minute.'

'I'll give it a try,' offered Jackson's desk partner, humbly, but with a look of excited intensity. Wing, standing nearby, gave Edward an encouraging pat on the shoulder.

'You'll be fine,' said Teddy. 'OK, that's still on, then. Right everyone, as they say here, "Toi, toi, toi" (sounded like 'toy'). Let's go.'

I looked at Freda, puzzled.

'Oh, it's a fancy way of saying "Good luck", which as you know, can bring bad luck. It's similar to "Break a leg" – not really appropriate in your case!' she said laughing, pointing to my bandaged foot.

Fabio took centre stage after the orchestra had settled and tuned up, and made announcements in Italian. I gathered he explained Jackson's absence, and raised a laugh at something he said about me, miming walking with crutches.

I hoped it was not too ridiculous. Finally he announced with a flourish of his arm the approach of Maestro Teddy Albright and, clapping towards Teddy as he passed him, left the stage. The audience applauded heartily. Then I hobbled on to make my introductory speech ...

I was grateful to Burney for providing me with the story about one of the evening's composers, Stradella. This character was also a singing teacher, taking on the children of the rich. He eloped with one of them, a young woman whose father was naturally outraged. So, he commissioned a couple of assassins to murder the upstart musician. They entered the church where Stradella was playing the organ and hid behind pillars. As he played, the thugs became so enchanted by his music, that they could not bring themselves to do the deed. Indeed, they warned him of the danger and urged him to escape. Unfortunately, some time later Stradella was assassinated by others employed by his former patron.

That got a laugh. Funny that. There's nothing comic about murder.

The concert was a huge success. Edward played the 'Devil's Trill' superbly, and received the deserved plaudits.

We were entertained at a reception after the concert provided by the British Council, the Italian Cultural Ministry and the province of Lazio. Prosecco flowed and nibbles greedily downed. By me, at least.

The British Ambassador was present and other notables, but the attention of most of the players was on two subjects: would the police capture the hijackers of the van, the instrument thieves, and where was Jackson?

CHAPTER 18

THE JOURNEY BACK by coach to the villa was passed largely in silence. There were some muted mutterings near us at first, in which the name 'Jackson' was mentioned, but the chatter fell away as collective tiredness washed over us, now the need to socialise had passed. I sat next to David, but shut my eyes and pretended to sleep. Really, I just did not want to talk to him.

When we arrived, David pecked me on the cheek and headed off towards his room, with a sad 'See you in the morning'. I joined some of the others clustered round the reception desk, asking for news of Jackson.

'Sorry, nothing.'

We turned as Teddy approached, and made way for him to approach the desk.

'This is worrying,' he said to Janet behind the desk counter. 'Have you checked his room? And the conference room – are his things just as he left them?'

'Yes' to both questions. The next piece of information woke me up.

Janet spoke loudly enough for us all to hear: 'We have contacted the police, and they say that if he has not returned by morning, they will come out and investigate. Meanwhile they are asking the local hospitals and other police services – there are so many in Italy – if he has turned up. So, try not to worry about it, and go and rest.'

Teddy looked as if he needed all he could get.

'I'll be back here at six tomorrow, OK? Meanwhile if or when he does show, please come and let me know at once.'

Pippa tugged at his sleeve, nodding with her head towards the Piazza Venezia, and we parted again to let them both pass. Just then, he turned and addressed us all.

'I'm sorry everyone. Shouldn't let this detract from what was a superb performance tonight. Well done. And thanks to Edward for stepping in so beautifully. When Jackson does turn up, he'll find he's not the only show in town!'

We tittered, not very enthusiastically. Something felt wrong, very wrong.

The next morning the whole company arrived early for breakfast. David was there, standing with Teddy in a corner of the room, both immersed in mobile conversations. Then they suddenly left, with Teddy signalling to Pippa to accompany them. I looked around at the subdued gathering. Robinson looked particularly distressed. Freda had her arm around him.

'Honest, honey. Don't get so worried. You know him. He'll be fine. Probably come back saying he'd stepped out for a smoke, met a beautiful young woman and gone off with her!'

Nice try, I thought. But it did not seem even remotely likely.

I munched my toast and cheese without tasting them, and considered all the possibilities of where Jackson had gone. Nobody around me spoke, until Naomi, on my right, asked 'I've packed, almost, but are we still going to Naples, or what, do you think?'

That was met with a shrugging of shoulders and shaking of heads. Nobody moved from their seats when they finished. We all sat, waiting for someone to tell us what to do next. Then Teddy and a party of people arrived, some in the uniform of police officers.

We turned towards them in silent concentration. Teddy lifted his hand to announce his speech:

'Listen up, everybody. The police here have been trying to trace Jackson ever since last night. No luck so far. It's usually too soon for them to start a missing person enquiry, but they realise the exceptional circumstances of this case. Jackson's things are still where he left them in the conference room after rehearsal yesterday, even his beloved Amati violin. So that area, and his room, are now considered out of bounds while the inspector here makes preliminary investigations.'

'Ispettoro di Maio, like the politico' the smiling policeman said, introducing himself. His reference was met with blank stares, none of us being too *au fait* with Italian politics. He went on, 'I am sorry, ladies and gentlemen of the orchestra, but you must all stay in this room and do not go to your bedrooms until I give the permission. OK?'

'Any questions?' asked Teddy.

A storm of voices arose. He picked out one question phrased in slightly different ways.

'I have cancelled the concert tonight in Naples. I know – huge disappointment. But until we know what's happened to one of our party, we really cannot continue with the plans. And no, I don't know when we'll be able to leave. It's all a mess, I realise, but we have to just sit tight and hope for the best.'

Philip Robinson stood up and all fell silent. He spoke, his voice shaking with emotion. 'Please, Teddy. Do they, the police, suspect foul play? I have to know.'

'Not yet, but it's too soon, and all too mysterious so far. They're going to bring dogs here, apparently. They'll trace Jackson's scent and hopefully find that he's just close by, no harm done, perhaps concussed. And who knows, in answer to the other question, if his disappearance is linked to the stealing of the instruments.'

He broke off to speak quietly with the officer, then turned and announced:

'Listen, I have Inspector Di Maio's permission for us to all go to the chapel, if you'd like, and I'll have the instruments brought there from the van. We'll play to take our minds off this, yes? There are the Jamelli and Piccini pieces to go over, just in case we do get to play them in Naples some time.'

The musicians left, chatting to each other in subdued tones. David went with them, talking to the head policeman as he went. I did not have my Naples script with me, so I stayed behind in the refectory with the TV crew.

Liz was standing in the corner excitedly shouting at her mobile to someone, presumably in London, asking what exactly was expected of her in the changing circumstances. Should the programme now switch its interest from music to missing persons?

Then David returned and sat beside me.

'I've offered to help, but it's tricky. There are already two police forces on the job: the state police, that's Di Maio, and the municipal police from Rocco di Papa, apparently a town nearby.'

Our attention was suddenly drawn to the window with the barking of dogs beyond.

'Ah, that must be the tracking dogs. Must go. See you later.'

I moved over to the huddle of silent and dejected technicians and sat opposite the blond man who had carried my suitcase when we had arrived. He told me a long rambling tale of how he had to be back on Sunday as he had another job to go to, filming fashion models in venues around London. 'Trust me to be stuck here,' was the gist of it. I let him go on as it seemed to relieve his tension, but barely listened. Another technician joined in, adding his tale of woe.

'I'm supposed to be helping the wife's mother move into a home next week. Can't do that if we're kept here by the police. What the hell is that Jackson Coen bloke thinking of, going AWOL. Something to hide, maybe.'

Just then Tina, the orchestra's librarian, entered and was soon doing her best to lighten the atmosphere by regaling Liz and the techies with stories of previous orchestral disasters.

She told them of the time during one of Teddy's concerts in St Petersburg, 'Music at the court of Catherine the Great'. The guest of honour, a political heavyweight, fell asleep and was heard by everyone snoring loudly.

Just then my mobile went off and all eyes fell on me.

'Yes, David? They've found him? What, already? Dead? Oh God, yes, will do.'

I apologized to the group and rang Teddy, telling him the news before anyone else did. Then we all sat in silence, taking in what we had dreaded.

'Bugger,' the blond sound technician broke in to our reverie. 'That'll screw us up here for days. Shit.' That summed up what I had been thinking.

CHAPTER 19

ONE AT A TIME we were sent for, leaving the comfort of the crowd in the refectory where we had been supplied with food, wine and jigsaw puzzles, for the intimidating process of being interviewed. David gave me his arm to lean on as I hobbled with just one crutch to the Cardinal Hume room – a large games room where a table tennis table had been requisitioned by interrogation officers. I was invited to sit on one side, with David beside me, as he had been with all the interviewees, and two men and a woman were sitting facing me. David supplied the introductions,

'This is Dottore Baletto, the Public Prosecutor who is leading the enquiry, and Commissario Bellini of the Judicial Police. Signora Berlusco will translate. This is my wife, Julia Deane. Not a musician but supplying the research.' The three B's is all I could think.

'Ah, yes, Signora Deane.' Baletto seemed to think I was a person of interest. That made me worry.

'Tell me. Why was you fight with Signor Coen?'

I must have looked nonplussed.

'In Padua. You have fight with him and he has *sangue e lividi* on his face.' His fingers fluttered around his cheek.

'Blood and bruises,' supplied Signora Berlusco.

'Oh that!' My stomach lurched. Did this make me a prime suspect? 'Oh nothing. Well,' that sounded stupid. You don't bash a man's face for nothing. 'No, actually, it was, erm, because he was too close, behind me.'

I turned to David for help, but he was just frowning with incomprehension. 'What I mean is, he was coming on to me, you know, sexually.' I gulped for air while the rather prim lady translator explained,

'*Venendo su di me, sessualmente.*'

'Ah' the two men exclaimed. All was made clear and simple. I thought it wise to add 'So, I had a glass of wine in my hand, and when I turned to repulse him, the glass caught his face. Accidentally, of course'.

There seemed no need to pursue this. They understood entirely. Even David looked relieved.

'Tell me, Signora, do you know anything, anyone who want to kill Signor Coen?'

I could think of several, but shook my head. Gossip is not helpful to a serious police enquiry, I told myself.

'He was not popular, but nobody I know, nobody here, could do that, I'm sure. Sorry I cannot help you.'

'Did you see anyone yesterday, Friday morning, after the *prova di musica*? Anyone not from the orchestra perhaps?'

'No,' I said, 'I was in bed until nearly lunchtime. Just back from the hospital and resting my damaged ankle. When I got up I just went downstairs. That's when I met David. I didn't notice anything strange.'

Something was nagging at the back of my mind, but nothing I could properly recall.

After the two Italian men spoke to each other, they looked at Signora Berlusco and said something which she relayed to me that it was over for now and I could leave.

She added: 'Please do not go to where the others are waiting. Go to another place. Do not talk to anybody about anything that was said in this room, OK?'

I nodded my assent. David gave me his arm and I hobbled out and towards my bedroom. I lay on the bed and rested my throbbing ankle, elbow and head. My thoughts and feelings were in a jumble and were only stilled when I dozed off. I must have been asleep for some time, because I woke with a jolt, suddenly aware of someone outside my door. Someone had stopped on the corridor and began singing, quite quietly but distinctly. I recognised the tune, 'La donna e mobile', from *Rigoletto*. It was as if the singer needed to practise just the first couple of lines, as he repeated them three or four times. I then heard, and saw, the doorhandle moving slowly. Thank God I had turned the lock on the inside. My body gave a deep shudder and turned icy cold. My mouth felt parched, but I croaked 'Hello?' There was no answer, but the sound of feet hurrying away.

I reached out for my mobile on the cabinet beside the bed and took a few deep breaths before pressing the speed dial for David. I must have controlled my voice from betraying anxiety as he replied, 'I'll be up as soon as I can,' he promised. 'Give me twenty minutes.'

After long minutes, by which time I had calmed my nerves, he appeared, carrying a tray of plates for my lunch. 'I was having mine when you called,' he explained.

While spaghetti slithered between my teeth, he updated me on the investigation. About half the people had been questioned, and nothing significant had come to light.

'Except,' he frowned, 'a detailed description from Freda of just how you came to be bashed on the head. Why on earth did you let her leave you there? Wouldn't limping on a sprained ankle be preferable to being shot – which you could have been?'

There was no answer to that. I just felt like a school kid being told off by an overbearing teacher. I changed the subject by telling him about the door handle fright.

'Right, that's it. We're moving you out of here. You'll have to share with me, whether you like it or not.'

For self-protection, I actually did. I finished my lunch while he made telephone arrangements with Janet. He stood up to take my tray, while speaking in a voice of restrained anger.

'We've got one of the double rooms in the suite, Piazza Venezia I think it's called. There are some steps to get to it, but I'm sure you'll manage. Now pack your things. Cosima will come to collect them to help you move. Meanwhile, keep the door locked and open it to no-one unless you're really sure who they are. You're always moaning about not having time to read, so here's your chance to get on with it.'

I preferred shouting to this quiet tone through almost clenched teeth. My own feelings were in turmoil, so why I decided this was the time to confess, I have no idea.

'Sit down, I have something to say.'

Puzzled, he placed the tray on the desk and sat down, staring at me. I felt a chill run through my skin.

'Now, you know, um, well, you had this affair ...'

He exploded. Shooting to his feet, 'Oh God. Here we go!'

'Wait, I … er …'

'No, you wait. That was over months ago. I've said I'm sorry.' He sighed impatiently. 'You know I really, really am. More than I can say.'

'Yes, well … but it was an affair. You had a relationship.'

'So? You know that.'

'Well, I thought our marriage was over, right?'

Strange silence. An icy breeze seemed to blow through the room.

'Why, you haven't …?'

'Just once,' I blurted. 'It wasn't serious, just once. And I was drunk! I didn't…'

'And who was it? Someone I know?'

'Fabio …'

'What? That gigolo? That cliché of a Latin lover?'

I felt trapped and did what I so despise, but was unable to prevent. I cried. At least there were tears coming from my eyes and rolling down my cheeks. I turned away, ashamed he should see my weak response. Then anger rose in me.

I turned back and shouted:

'Well, I thought it was over! You did that. You did. Don't go blaming me for reacting.'

He turned to the desk and picked up the tray. Then put it down again. He looked at me as if working out what he should say. Then he stepped over to the bed, knelt down beside it and took my hands in his.

'I know, Julia. And I'm sorry. You don't know how sorry I am. I have always loved you and always will. You mustn't think that that other woman meant anything to me. It was a weakness. I was on my own …'

I stared at him, sobbing quietly. 'Don't ...'

'No, listen. When I was starting in a new place, not knowing anyone, she was really helpful. Sylvia, her name. She worked in the forensic laboratory and I happened to go there quite a bit over some evidence that was proving difficult. She invited me out, for a meal, and I couldn't see what was wrong with that. You used to go out for meals with colleagues of yours at Queen's'.

'Yes, but I didn't go to bed with them, or call them "Darling"!'

'Well you weren't there! It was months before you moved in fully. Just seeing you at odd weekends wasn't enough. I was lonely, she was too – her husband had died the year before – and we enjoyed each other's company. Then, well, it just happened. Then it kind of, couldn't stop. But I never felt unfaithful, not really. You were still the only one. My wife of ten years.'

I pursed my lips. Should I make it easy for him, after all the months of heartbreak I had gone through? Was I just to forgive him?

Then I remembered what Father Hayes had told me, about the wealthy Liverpool philanthropist whose guests left after being offered a poor meal, leaving only his real friends.

Was this the poor meal in our relationship, and was I one of those not prepared to stay on to enjoy the secret second meal, the real feast? Was I jumping ship at the first big wave? Anyway, I realised, I had just confessed to adultery myself. Maybe I should be prudent.

'All right, but let's start again. Don't take me for granted. Let's go easy until we can both feel comfortable – or not.'

'Fair enough. OK. Now I'm going but I'll be back later.

There's no point in your leaving this room. All the others in the house are either in their rooms or waiting to be interviewed. Ring me if you need anything, and let Cosima in when she comes for your things.'

I collected up my goods, throwing them in the suitcase or my backpack, and watched when, later, Cosima drew all my clothes from the wardrobe, clutched them to her, and also carried my case.

CHAPTER 20

WHEN DAVID CAME FOR ME, I had only my backpack to put on and to arrange my arms onto the crutches. My room, number 64, was the last on the corridor. Through a further door was the passageway leading to the conference room. So I asked David to show me the scene of the crime, if that would be permitted. He nodded, and led the way, going as far as the police tape allowed. We stood at the end of the corridor and watched two figures encased in white nylon from their head to below their feet, who were on their knees on the marble flags of the square hallway. They were studying the ground in minute detail for anything it might show.

'Hi,' called David, and 'Ciao!' they responded, continuing their tasks.

David and I craned our heads to the left, beyond the conference room and the hallway, towards the outside door.

'They've already tested for blood and found lots of traces just here and in the wash basin.' David said, pointing to the floor and to the toilets. 'They're still looking for the weapon.

Whoever did it made a thorough job of cleaning up, using water and the paper towels. The officers found lots of blood-soaked paper towels near the body. They're checking them for DNA.'

'Where was the body?'

'Just out there, down in one of the caves; the nearest one, behind the statue of Our Lady. It goes back into the rock quite a way but the body was near the entrance. It must have been quite a job for the killer to drag it outside, up and over the wall, across the platform and down into the cave. He was no lightweight, that Jackson Coen. Whoever killed him must have called on someone to help, unless there were always two working together. There was blood on the floor here with a trail leading right up to the cave, but they could not really see it all until the light scanner showed it up.'

Just then someone opened the outer door as we were looking in that direction. The forensic officers stood up and invited two uniformed officers to enter the hallway, saying something to them in Italian. Then a couple of excited dogs, like blood hounds, followed, pulling a red-faced older man on their leashes. The three policemen and the dogs exited through the door to our right, which led down steps to the courtyard below.

As the white-clad investigators joked about the dogs' antics, another officer arrived, a young woman wearing a beaming smile and a similar full white body suit, only hers was besmirched with dirt, dust and blood. She appeared in the hallway holding what looked like a heavy and blood-stained stone artefact about eighteen inches in length. It was shaped like the pedestal of a narrow column. With two hands she held it aloft as a trophy.

'I recognize that,' I exclaimed. 'It's the doorstop. Last time I saw it, it was there, near the door to the conference room. I thought when I saw it, only in Italy could you have something that looks like an antique being used as a doorstop.'

There was none of the gaiety and chatter of previous meals at supper. Voices were subdued and faces impassive. Even Freda lacked her usual ebullience and Teddy looked grey and haggard. Someone among us could be a killer, I told myself with a shiver. Or even more than one. And possibly a van-jacker and instrument thief too.

Looking around at the diners, I assessed who among them had some sort of motive to do away with Jackson, but that seemed to cover nearly everyone present, and none of them appeared to me to be capable of such a grotesque act. Of course, it could have been an outsider, someone connected with the Mafia. Maybe Jackson had surprised one of them, maybe the person trying my door handle, and been done to death to shut him up. Maybe he was even somehow involved – although with his own precious violin at risk, that was hardly likely.

One of the TV crew made a joke to his neighbour about something, but was quickly shamed into silence by shushes and black looks.

A uniformed policeman hovered around the door.

'He's been posted to keep an eye on us,' David explained. 'He's to make sure no-one enters the conference area or Jackson's bedroom. Forensics have finished, but it's still a crime scene.'

After supper everyone dispersed quietly to their rooms. I

went with David to the Piazza Venezia, and we spent an hour supposedly watching television in the small living area along with Teddy and Pippa, and Tina and Jeremy, the other couple using this suite of double rooms.

We made occasional desultory conversation, none of us properly watching the Italian game show on the screen, but I, at least, grateful for it filling the gaps of silence.

After the other two couples bade their goodnights, we entered our room. Cosima had not only brought down my suitcase, but hung up my clothes in the wardrobe too. After some awkwardness, we got into bed and clung to our outside edges, trying to avoid touching the other. I don't know what happened during the night to change that, but I found myself next morning with my head on David's shoulder, and his arm around me. I gently extracted myself while he slept on. From the shower I could hear his mobile ring tone. Then his voice raised in a 'Good God, no!'

I draped my wet body in a towel and went into the bedroom to find David already out of bed and half dressed.

'You won't believe this,' he said, pulling a shirt off its hanger. 'There's been another incident. A body, well – that double-bass player.'

'Nelson!' I almost screamed. 'No. What? What's happened?'

'He's been stabbed, possibly dead. Must go. You stay here until you're called for. The place will soon be swarming with even more police and they'll not want musicians clogging up the scene.'

I had to sit down on the bed to take in what I had heard.

Nelson, that lovely gentle man. Then I remembered that it was Nelson I had seen hurrying down my corridor roughly the time when Jackson had been killed. Nelson with his enormous bass case almost running down the corridor. I had forgotten to mention that to the Public Prosecutor.

My God. My body shuddered and then suddenly flushed with heat. Did that omission somehow cause Nelson to be attacked? Am I in a way responsible for that?

I felt an urgent need to tell someone, a police officer.

I dressed, almost as quickly as David had, grabbed my crutches and swung myself down the steps of the Piazza Venezia and into the cloister, wet hair sticking to my scalp and dripping onto my collar.

At the far end, beyond the reception desk, there were people thronging and rubber-necking between the door to the chapel and the entrance to the underpass. David and the uniformed policeman were physically moving them away, shouting at them to disperse.

'This is a crime scene,' I heard David call angrily. 'Go and have your breakfast! Stay in the dining room.'

Alongside the reception desk was a smaller group. As I approached them I could see that Freda was sitting on one of the knee-high window ledges that lined one side of the cloister. She was visibly upset and being comforted by Pippa and Naomi. Teddy, Wing and a couple of others were standing by.

Suddenly two television cameramen pushed by me, capturing all the excitement on video. Liz followed, with the sound engineer holding up a large furry microphone. They lingered a little on Freda's group then moved along to where David and the policeman were securing the scene. I was disgusted, almost nauseous. How could they film genuinely-felt grief, and intrude into the shock we were feeling? Is nothing sacred, nothing private? I fisted my hands in rising anger. Freda, seeing me nearby, quickly stood, rushed to me and flung her arms around me.

'Oh Julia, sweetie. This is just too awful. Too bloody awful!'

Teddy and Pippa went off as I sat Freda back down, and with my arm around her shoulder, and Naomi holding her hand, asked her what had happened. Wing hovered around, looking concerned, and David stood nearby, listening intently.

I could feel Freda shaking, her usually indomitable frame crumpled and weak, and tears coursed down her cheeks. I held back her long blonde hair so that it should not stick to her face with salty water.

'What happened?' David asked softly.

'I was coming to breakfast,' she sniffed, 'and met Robinson coming down the stairs from the new block, where you stayed until you moved. You know the sign on the chapel door asks you not to go through the chapel but to use the underpass? I made a joke to him, something about needing the exercise, and went down the stairs. I prefer that route to going through the chapel. Sometimes that priest is in there, praying, and I don't like to disturb him.'

'You both went down, you and Robinson?' I asked, pointlessly. It gave her a chance to blow her nose and wipe her face.

'Well, I was ahead of him. So, when we turned into the brick tunnel, it was me who saw him first – Nelson. Just lying there, face down. I thought for a moment he had tripped, or was asleep. Of course, when I saw the knife I just screamed. It was sticking out of his back.'

She became overcome at the memory and I let her take great sobbing breaths, giving her a gentle squeeze. Naomi made soothing sounds of the 'It's OK' variety. In a few moments Freda recovered sufficiently to continue, and I thought it was probably good for her to be able to describe it all. She would have to repeat all this anyway to the police.

'I just stood there,' she said. 'Robinson was wonderful; he did what he could. He turned Nelson over. Of course, he had to take the knife out first, and then he gave him mouth-to-mouth, just in case there was a chance he could recover.' She paused, frowning with the effort of remembering. 'It was one of those sharp fruit knives – more like serrated steak knives – that they give us at dinner.'

We looked around at each other, then back to Freda, who continued, 'He was wonderful, Robinson. The only time he broke off from trying to save Nelson was to tell me to go get someone, get help. I left him and ran as fast as I could out this end of the underpass, and Cosima met me. She had heard me scream and was coming to see what was happening. She went straight and phoned the cops and your David. God, I'm going to be sick.'

I had been so keen to hear her story I had not thought of Freda's immediate welfare. Rather than face everyone in the dining room, Naomi and I took her between us to the Internet café where I had been brought injured just a couple of days before. Wing put the kettle on and made Freda a mug of sweet tea, while Naomi and I sat her down on one of the woven wicker chairs.

CHAPTER 21

THE REST OF THAT MORNING was spent hanging around waiting for, or being interviewed by, the Public Prosecutor, this time with an extra plain-clothed detective whose name I did not catch. Most of us, orchestra and television crew, at least had the pleasure of sitting on the outside terrace in the sunshine while waiting for our turn.

Simon and Jude must have quarrelled as they were sitting separately. Jude was talking quietly with Naomi, while Simon was on his own. I drew up a chair next to Simon and he smiled sadly at me.

'Problem?' I asked.

'Yeah, Jude's a prick. He is still in touch with his previous partner. Caught him sending him pictures of himself. We had a massive row.'

'Will you forgive him?'

'S'pose so, if he promises not to do it again. But what of you and your husband – are you back together? Have you forgiven him?'

Ow, that hurt. Had I? That was too close to the story of the philanthropist's guests which was already probing my conscience. Was forgiveness the answer? Would it blank out the past, or simply serve as a temporary truce while storing up the hurt in an account to be drawn on whenever I wanted to feel wronged or vengeful? I changed the subject, turned it back to Simon.

'Have you someone in your past you had to forgive? Apart from Jude just now?'

'Yes, actually. Mark, my previous partner. He went off with Jude's guy. That's how we met. We were the rejects! My partner, Mark, played in a Quartet we made up after college. It was really good, but obviously we broke-up when he went off with Josh. But he taught me something. It was his love of animals.'

I was intrigued. That was a great cause of mine, but I failed to see a connection.

'Go on,' I urged, 'how did that help?'

'He taught me to see how we use animals as things to help us, please us, entertain us, you know?'

'Yeah, I do.'

'Well, if we judge animals by how they relate to us, setting ourselves up as sort of idols or gods to be served by them, not respecting them in their own right, as their own creatures … that's unjust, yes?'

'Yes, indeed.' I was really warming to Simon for expressing this.

'Well, it made me think that maybe I was treating Mark like that, seeing his life only as it related to me. Then I thought that love, real love, should disregard that and see his life as having value to him, so that his need to find happiness some-where else, not with me, shouldn't get to me. I should let him be happy however it made me feel. D'you see what I mean?'

'I do,' I said, frowning with the mental effort of translating his relationship to mine. Stop it. 'But what about Jude now. Aren't you putting your feelings before him?'

'Well, Mark was straight with me when we broke up. He told me that he was finding Jude's guy's company great and would like to start a relationship with him. He said he thought ours was getting rather stale, but Mark didn't mean he would stop loving me, just that he did not want to be with me all the time. I kind of understood that. But Jude is messing me about with still keeping in touch with his ex and not letting me know. And what about Mark? He's being hurt now as his partner is still messing about with Jude. It's a mess, but it's the dishonesty that hurts. I thought Jude was better than that. But, of course I'll forgive him. I love him. Simples, as the advert has it.'

I felt as I do at a Service of Reconciliation, when the priest calls out a list of things we might have to feel guilty about, such as driving impatiently, or gossiping maliciously. Some on the list do niggle my conscience; in my case usually sins of omission, such as not visiting an elderly neighbour or not helping out at a food bank. This one now was 'Have I put my feelings of hurt before those of forgiveness and love?' Not to mention 'Am I making myself a drama queen and parading my innocent victimhood, rather than accepting that the man I chose to love for a lifetime is human and fallible and makes mistakes, as do I?'

Hell. That's a lot to take in. And at a time when two of our own have been brutally murdered. I sat blank-faced, my mind wandering through a labyrinth of thoughts.

A young uniformed policeman was standing guard at the door, checking that no-one attempted an escape. I watched him, with his impassive expression, and wandered if he too had a complicated love life, or perhaps he lived in an ideal blessedness in which nothing ever went wrong. Did that stern face smile tenderly at his beloved every night? Did he call her pet names and take his time in bed until she was ready? Simon was watching me eyeing the young policeman. When I looked back, we both smiled in silent understanding.

There were only three ways anybody could escape from the terrace. One was by going through the building and out through the front entrance. Or someone coud go through the fire door by the chapel into the courtyard, accessed as well by walking around the side of the building through the narrow path. Beneath the near end of the new wing, furthest from the conference centre, is an archway with an outside gate. Otherwise, the only way out was at the far end of the garden, via the spiral rock-hewn staircase up onto the field and into the woods. None of these routes were feasible with all the police officers around, so the cold-blooded killer was still among us and would continue to be until he, or she, was arrested.

I looked around to see if anyone was looking unnaturally nervous or edgy. No-one did. They were all just sitting placidly in the autumn sunshine, reading or chatting, or snoozing with bared skin in the hope of a tan.

Another officer appeared at the door, a uniformed woman with long wavy hair pulled back under a peaked cap, wearing a pencil-tight skirt and high heels. She called out the name of one of us for interview, accompanying him or her inside the building and reappearing after several minutes to call for the next.

Neither Freda nor Robinson were with us, so I had no doubt they were the first to be interrogated. Teddy and Pippa were called together from the terrace, followed by each of the film crew in turn, with Liz the last. Then Simon's friend Jude followed, with Naomi and Wing going shortly after. My name was called. I stuffed the book I had been trying to read, without great success, into my bag, grabbed the crutches and hobbled along behind the policewoman into the same Cardinal Hume games room which had been used for the earlier interview. David smiled and asked how I was before introducing me to the third interrogator. The same woman translator was making notes.

Before being asked a question, I blurted out that I had remembered something that might be of real importance. Five pairs of eyes, four Italian and one English, fixed me with piercing stares.

'You know you asked me yesterday if I saw anyone behaving strangely on the Friday morning at the time of Jackson's murder?'

Not that they had used those words. Two heads nodded.

'Well, I had been in my room, number 64, after coming back from the hospital. Some of the musicians had been with me, but they left me to rest. I know that Teddy Albright left me about eleven o'clock to finish off the rehearsal in the conference room. Then the others went and I fell asleep. When I came to ...' I had to stop to let the translator explain what I had said, 'I left my bedroom to go to lunch. When I went into the corridor, I saw Nelson – just a glimpse of him – carrying his giant bass case, ahead of me. He disappeared round the corner, you know the corridor goes into a sharp bend before straightening out again. I had to go back into my room to get my performance clothes, and by the time I was in the corridor again, he had gone.'

'So he was going away from the conference room?'

'Yes.'

'And what time was this?'

'It must have been about half-past twelve as I wanted to catch some sun on the terrace before lunch at one.'

'So you came down the stairs alone?'

'Yes, using the stairlift chair. I had the remote so could operate it.'

'And when did you next see Nelson?'

'I don't know. I suppose at lunchtime. I don't remember. I had just met David. Yes, it was. He arrived in the dining room, or refectory, whatever you call it, a little late because he sat at the end of the table, I remember now.'

David nodded in agreement. 'Yes, I saw him there too. It struck me that he was the only black man in the orchestra.'

'How did he seem? Agitated?'

Both David and I shook our heads, and said, almost in chorus, 'Sorry, can't say.'

Then I spoke, 'I had not expected to see David here, so was preoccupied. Sorry.'

'Do you want to say anything else that can help us? Anything at all about Nelson? We know that he and Jackson Coen had an argument. Nelson's son was arrested, yes? For drugs — and the father, he blamed Jackson, right?'

I nodded. 'That's all I know. I think Nelson's son was fined and given a suspended sentence, but am not sure. I heard it from someone as it didn't seem …'

'We understand. Right, thank you Mrs, sorry, *Dottoressa* Deane. You can go, but please don't say nothing to the people outside, OK? Do not go again to the terrace and do not try to leave the building.'

David took my hand and gently pressed it, while giving me an encouraging smile. I manoeuvred the crutches and made for the door.

'Please, if you remember something else. Anything at all, you will come back here immediately, yes?'

I nodded in agreement and left for the Hinsley sitting room. Something was troubling me, but I could not identify what. Maybe Nelson was not alone. There could have been someone with him, in front of him, but I could not be sure.

CHAPTER 22

BY LUNCHTIME EVERYONE had been questioned. We were all sitting down in the refectory ready to be served when Teddy announced that the forensic team wanted DNA swabs and fingerprints taken from everyone after lunch. They also wanted us to hand over the clothes we were wearing or had been wearing earlier that morning. We would be allowed to go to our rooms after lunch to change our clothes and then take the ones we had been wearing to the room where the interviews had been. A team would be there from one-thirty onwards.

The mood in the room was gloomy. David came to sit beside me, and Freda was sitting opposite.

'I can't believe this. It's all so weird and terrible,' she said, summing-up my feelings exactly.

Naomi next to her added, 'I just can't believe that one of us can be a killer – and twice over.'

'Poor Gillian,' added Simon the cellist, the other side of

Freda. I must have looked quizzical, for he added, 'Nelson's wife, y'know.'

I had not thought that each person present was the centre of their own world of relationships, of networks and contacts. Of course they were. The death of anyone causes grief to spread over many overlapping circles. We finished our meals in silence.

David helped me to our room in the Piazza Venezia, which was near to the dining room. I took off my blouse and skirt and found others in the wardrobe. David was looking out of the window overlooking the garden terrace when he called out 'Hey! Who's that?'

I joined him and watched as a man, with a small suitcase in one hand and a violin case in the other, was walking with rapid steps up the avenue in the garden. He looked back, I saw the black beard and recognised him as Edward, the player who replaced Jackson two nights before in the 'Devil's Trill'.

David did not wait to be told. He flew out of the room and, as I continued to watch, he reappeared moments later below me in the garden followed closely by a uniformed policeman. Edward turned, saw them and began to run. They raced to catch the fugitive. Damn those trees! I could not see the moment of capture as a row of cypress tress blocked the view of the end of the garden, where the rocky stairway would provide an escape.

In short order the two law-officers: David and the policeman, reappeared, walking towards the villa with a dejected-looking Edward firmly held between them.

In his free hand David carried the violin case and the policeman held the suitcase. They passed into the doorway out of my sight and I sat on the bed to recover my thoughts.

Edward. Could it be he? Was he the murderer both of Jackson and of Nelson? Had Nelson seen him kill Jackson and so had to be silenced? I remembered hearing something about there being bad blood between Edward and Jackson over a recording contract. Maybe if a lot of money is involved, or professional reputation, that is enough to kill someone. But what could Nelson have to do with that? Edward had seemed such a pleasant, easy-going person. Could even the mildest of men plunge a knife into someone's back or smash a person over the head?

I shook myself mentally. Concentrate on the concrete, not speculation, I told myself. Now that someone has been captured, was it still necessary to produce my clothing and have a DNA swab?

Possibly, so I gathered up my morning's clothes and, with only one crutch, limped out and down the dozen steps from Piazza Venezia into the cloister heading towards the Cardinal Hume interview room. There was a stream of people already either ahead of me or behind me, each carrying clothing or bags of clothing, and all making for the place we had been told to go to. Just as the first of our party arrived at the door, it opened and the uniformed policewoman with the high heels came out, closing it behind her. She held up her hand to demand attention, and in a clear voice ordered,

'Tutti voi vi fermate. Tornano indietro. C'è stato uno sviluppo,' she said, then attempted a translation at the sight of our mystified expression, 'Is a devellomento.'

'There's been a development,' Freda's voice boomed out. 'She says she wants us all to go back.'

They all stopped dead. Silence. Then suddenly:

'What?'

'What's happened?'

'Has someone confessed?'

'Is it one of us?'

I was unsure whether or not to divulge what I had seen, but could not resist.

'Yes,' I said, suddenly the centre of attention. 'Edward has been arrested ...'

They all turned to face me with expressions of shock or disbelief. Just then David emerged from the Hume room and stood beside the policewoman.

'Would you all go back,' he commanded, 'and please be quiet. Return to your rooms or go onto the terrace, and we'll contact you when there is anything you or we need to know ... And yes, it's true. We're holding Edward as a suspect. Now that's all I'm going to say. We may need your clothes, so hold on to them.'

He returned to the room and the policewoman ushered us away with sweeping gestures. Freda caught my eye, and I invited her to come back with me into the Piazza Venezia.

When we got to the suite's small living area, Teddy and Pippa were there boiling some water on the stove and clanking mugs. Tina and Jeremy emerged from their room to join us. Freda let me update them. All I could say was that Edward had been trying to leave the grounds, no doubt through the rock staircase, but after David had spotted him through the window he was caught by him and a policeman. Teddy looked shattered, and lowered himself onto the sofa.

'I had no idea. Of course, I knew he hated Jackson, as did a lot of the players, but not to that extent.'

'The record contract?'

'Perhaps ... Oh my God, and the fact that Jackson got the job – the one teaching composition and theory at the Royal College. They were both after that, but — Ha!' His eyes widened and sparkled with pleasure. 'Oh Good Lord, oh wonders!' He beamed around, catching up Pippa's hand. 'Where are the police? All in the Hume room?'

With impressive energy, he bounded up. 'Come on,' he ordered Pippa. 'We can clear this up. Edward was with us at the time we presume Jackson was being killed, remember? After the rehearsal we came back here with him and discussed the running order of the programme. D'you remember he thought the Naples programme would overrun and we discussed what we could drop from it? We went straight on to lunch after that and that's when we first noticed that Jackson was not there. Remember?'

She nodded, also cheering up.

'So, we're his alibi.'

With a broad smile, Teddy led Pippa by the hand and they hurried down the stairs. Tina and Jeremy smiled at each other and at me.

'I'm so glad it can't have been Edward,' Tina said quietly. 'Let's go and sit outside.'

She and Jeremy left, and Freda made us both some instant coffee with the now-boiling water. We sat for a while on the sofa, sipped our drinks and mused over the events.

'Why, if he was innocent, did he run?'

'Maybe he didn't kill Jackson, but was involved in the robbery.'

'Or maybe he killed Nelson, but not Jackson.'

'Maybe Nelson killed Jackson.'

'Maybe the Mafia ...'

I felt exhausted, and after Freda left to join the others on the terrace, I went to my room, put the clothing down that I had collected for the police, and lay on the bed.

While I was trying to sort out all the conflicting and confusing thoughts, I heard a voice in the living area outside the room singing the first two lines of 'La Donna e mobile'. This has happened before, I vaguely remembered. The singer stopped after the two lines, and sang them again, as if he could not remember the rest.

'Shut up, bloody musicians,' I muttered, 'I need to think.'

I closed my eyes but could not rest, so got up, hobbled over to the chest of drawers and tidied up a few of the items strewn around. I read through the notes for my talk for the Naples concert and put them in a drawer in the desk, thinking that they may now never be used. The desk was underneath the window from which I had earlier seen Edward attempting to flee.

Hearing voices below me on the terrace, I looked out and saw Tina and Jeremy were sitting at a table chatting with Freda. Simon, Jude and one of the television men were at another. Frank was on his own, as was Liz. She, head back and arms stretched in front of her, was soaking up the sunshine. He, with sunglasses and hat, was buried deep in a book. I felt a fool for being indoors when I too could have been out there. So, I grabbed my crutches and made my way down the steps into the corridor leading out to the terrace.

A tune was running through my head. By the time I emerged into the sunshine and approached the nearest occupied table, I was still trilling what sounded like, 'La donn' ay mobillay, Tacherey oppoorey, la la la dadda da, la la la dadda da.'

Freda was sitting with her back to me, and swung round suddenly,

'Hi, honey! What was that? Sing that again!'

I was flattered that she thought my voice worth hearing again, so did as she asked.

'La donn'ay mobillay, tacherey oppoorey.'

'Oh my God!' she said with wide opened eyes. Her hand suddenly covered her mouth.

'It's not that bad,' I said.

'No, it's what you sang.' She stood up and pulled my arm to take me out of earshot of the others. 'You remember what I said about the sign T next to you in the woods, and the sock in your mouth?'

I nodded, beginning to feel frightened.

'You were singing that line from *Rigoletto*, 'La Donna e mobile,' but the next one should have been *Qual piuma al vento*. What you were singing was *Tacere oppure*. Remember? Be quiet or else! A rather literary way of saying shut up. The more usual would be something like *stai zitto o altro* or *silenzio o altro*.

I did not think this was the time for a lesson in the finer points of Italian.

'Where did you get that *Tacere oppure* line from – or did you remember it from when I told you it was what the T meant?'

She looked incredulous. She was right to look so. My memory was not so good, although with a head wound, funny things can happen.

'No,' I said with a sudden realization. 'I've heard it sung a couple of times. Outside my door when I was in number 64 and someone was repeating it just now in the room in the Piazza Venezia. Where we had coffee.'

'Just now? Hey, Frank, you recently came past the Piazza Venezia. Did you see anyone coming out from it, or going in?'

Frank looked up from his book and shook his head.

'No, sorry. Didn't see anyone.'

At that moment Fabio appeared, someone I had not seen for a while. He must have just gone past the door to the Piazza Venezia. My heart pounded. Could he have stepped into the Internet café next door after leaving the Piazza Venezia, and now come out as if nothing had happened?

Freda and I both looked at each other for a moment in silence. Then Freda, being Freda, threw her arms around me in bear hug.

'Don't worry, sweetie. Don't worry.'

When she unwound herself from me, she still held my upper arms. 'We'll go find David, right now. The guy can't be far away.'

We knocked first but then burst into the Hume interview room, where police were clustered around the table and Edward was sitting looking dejected. David stood up at once and bundled us out through the door, turning back to explain to Italian colleagues that he would be only a minute, but that this matter must be important.

The three of us made quickly for the nearest comfortable space, the mercifully empty Internet café. Freda reminded David about the original 'Be quiet or else' business. Then she left it to me to tell him of the singer's sinister message couched in the made-up words of the Verdi aria.

David said nothing but looked thoughtful and worried. I too was feeling worried. My safety was at stake, yet I was also distracted by seeing Edward's face in my mind and felt suddenly painfully sorry for him. Why, I wondered, did he still look so miserable if Teddy had provided an alibi?

'What's happened about Edward? Did Teddy tell you he was with them?'

'Yes, he did. It seems Edward had nothing to do with Jackson's death. About Nelson's, we can't be sure.'

'Why did he run?' Freda came right to the point.

'OK, I'll tell you. But don't go spreading it.'

We assured him of our utter discretion.

'It seems Edward was out here, in Italy, Naples, some years ago, as were several of this band, playing in some opera company there. In 2005 I think he said. One night he went with a young man to the youth's apartment. I don't need to tell you what they were up to.'

Always so delicate, David. Leaving everything to my imagination.

'Anyway, it seems the young man had a heart attack, or fit or something, during one of their sex games, and Edward just ran away. Scared he'd be accused of killing him, which he may well have done, we just don't know. The case will have to be reopened. Anyway, when everyone here was about to be tested for DNA and fingerprints, he felt the police would find the link to this old case and get him for it. That's why he ran. Sudden impulse of panic, apparently.'

It made sense. David then changed his expression to one of concern for me, concentrating his gaze on my face.

'Going back to the incident in the woods. Can you

remember anything at all about the men who were arguing? Did you see any of them, or recognise a voice? It seems whoever stole the van knew it contained incredibly expensive instruments. Especially Jackson's, apparently. There could well have been an inside tip-off. Think, Julia.'

I did that. I rummaged around in the deepest recesses of my memory.

'What I remember is that we were in the woods, taking a breather, when we heard voices and Freda ...' I looked at her and we both smiled. I continued, 'Freda wanted to eavesdrop, just for fun ...' she nodded, vigorously.

'Oh God, I wish I hadn't.' She sounded as if she meant that.

'We got a bit closer to the trees and bushes that were between us and the men who were talking. Arguing really, talking loudly, angrily. I think there were three blokes. One I could see, short man, swarthy, dark scruffy hair. He may have been carrying a motorbike helmet.'

'Really?'

'I saw a couple of motorbikes, in an area of grassland behind where the men were. It was not far from the road.'

'Who else was there?'

'There was a second chap, with his back to me. I could sort of see him, but don't remember anything about him. And the third man was completely hidden from my view.'

David looked at Freda.

'Same here. I could see the guy with the helmet under his arm. Wore blue jeans and a dark blue shirt, opened to his belly button. Hairy chest. That's all I could see. He was waving his free arm in the direction of the guy with his back to me. All I could see of him was he was tall and was wearing a baseball cap, red, I think. The third guy was hidden behind a tree or something, and he was yelling at the other two, sounded really angry. Till he said *"Zitto"*, kind of Italian for "shut up". That's when I guessed they'd heard or noticed us and we beat it out of there.'

'Could you hear anything of what they were saying?'

Freda continued, 'I did hear the Italian words for "instruments" and "police" and "operation" and guessed they were discussing the heist of our van and gear.'

'And you?' David turned to me.

'Only voices. I couldn't tell what they were saying. But the hidden one sounded like …' My voice trailed off because I did not want to give my opinion. It was only an impression. I had no proof.

'Do you think,' asked David with that intense look he gets when he has an idea, 'that the voice of the hidden man could be the same as that of the person singing outside your door?'

I frowned. So did Freda.

'Well, yes, I suppose it could be.'

'Right. Stay there, talk to no-one about this. I'm going back to have a word with Judge Baletto. I know he's investigating the two murders, but they might be connected with the van-jacking. Make yourselves some tea while you're waiting.'

David has to micromanage. Making tea is something I do not have to be told to do. Freda brought over two steaming mugs as I sat on one chair and rested my damaged foot on another. We just sipped in silence, wondering what would happen next. Simon and Jude came in, laughing at some private joke. They had obviously made up. I was so pleased for them.

'Hi girls,' Simon greeted us, smiling. He took out a couple

of mugs and went about making tea or coffee, while Jude sat in front of one of the computer screens and began working at it. Simon sat alongside him and the two drank and joked as they followed something on the screen that must have been amusing to them.

CHAPTER 23

AFTER TEN MINUTES OR SO, David returned and invited Freda and me to go with him to the Hume room. Just outside it, he whispered to us,

'Go along with whatever happens now. This could lead to a breakthrough.'

Intrigued, we entered, and two uniformed police officers stood up at once and invited us into the far corner of the room, where two chairs had been placed.

Freda and I sat in them, while a folding screen was brought into the room and placed in front of us, blocking our view of the rest of the room. We turned to each other quizzically.

'How weird is this?' laughed Freda.

David appeared around the screen.

'OK, this is the plan. We're going to bring in all the men whose movements were not accounted for on the Thursday morning when you were in the woods. There were some who spent the time on the terrace, or were practising in the chapel, and were seen by others. But of the rest, they're going to sing for you. Freda, you can tell if a voice is false, can't you? Not the natural one, if someone is deliberately altering their normal singing voice?'

'I guess so,' she agreed, smiling, as David retreated beyond the screen. Freda and I listened to the muted voices of the several Italians in the room, as the police and the prosecutor were arranging themselves to be witnesses to this experiment. David and the translator were talking quietly together, and then Teddy's voice was added. I could make out certain names being recited from a list, with comments from Teddy.

'Sorry about the delay, ladies,' David shouted.

'It's OK, and we can hear pretty well here,' answered Freda.

More whispering, door opening and closing, feet shuffling, chair scraping. Freda and I looked at each other and giggled.

Finally, David's voice came over at normal volume.

'Right, please would you look over there, towards the screen, and sing the words you see on the paper. Do not say a word, please, just sing. This isn't an audition, just humour me, please.'

A tenor voice set off:

La Donna e mobile,
   Qual piuma al vento
   Muta d'accento
   E di pensiero.

'OK, thank you. That's all for that song, although we may ask for it again. Now, will you read this, in as angry a voice as you can, please.'

The unseen speaker, whom I judged to be either Simon or Jude, struggled to read a speech in Italian. He gave up after a few tries.

'Sorry, my Italian is rubbish. I know the song, heard it often enough, but can't read or speak it.'

'That's fine, thank you. You can go, but I must insist you say nothing of what you have been asked to do in here. We're going to put several blokes through it, and don't want anyone preparing themselves, OK?

'Yeah, sure.'

David appeared from in front of the screen as the first victim left the room.

'Well? You see how it goes. Obviously, he's not our man in the woods. But is he the singer?'

'No, the voice I heard was lower, more baritone. And the more I think of it, the more I believe it was the same as the voice in the woods.' I was really sure of that now.

'That's a really cool idea. What is on the paper he tried to read from?' Freda asked.

'Just a speech the translator and I cooked up to resemble – without giving too much away – what the man you couldn't see in the woods was likely to be saying. If you think, either of you, that you recognise his voice, don't say anything at the time. Wait for me to look round. If you want something repeated, just mouth it and I'll make them do it.'

We nodded, and he went back to his post. The next voice was by another tenor. It was trained and mellifluous and I guessed it belonged to Vaclav. I shook my head vigorously when David's face appeared. The singer did not have to read the speech.

The third voice sobered me. I began to shake. Freda, ever sensitive, placed her hand on mine. I nodded to David and the speech was read, with suitable expression. It sounded authentically Italian. Freda looked troubled, and I saw her shake her head slightly. When David looked round again, I nodded, but she shook her head more decidedly. David frowned and withdrew. He asked the singer to leave, and admonished him not to say anything, as he had the previous two, then he said something under his voice to somebody else.

A fourth man, I imagine one of the television crew, was next. His total lack of Italian ruled him out.

The fifth man sounded like Edward. He must have been shaking, as a cracked and reedy voice wobbled over the first few notes. He broke down sobbing before he reached the end of the stanza. Freda and I shook our heads. No way.

I thought I had already detected the voice of the singer but was struck when the next one began by how it seemed to be the perfect fit. My eyebrows shot up to my hairline, and Freda's creased into a frown. We nodded to David. As the singer began to read off the speech, my heart stopped beating, and Freda gasped, 'My God!'

As the speaker continued speaking, in admirable Italian but with little emotion, I am sure my hands felt clammy, and my mouth went dry. The next time David's face appeared, Freda and I nodded vigorously. He put his finger to his lips and I could hear the speaker leaving and a few minutes later another taking his place, as a deep bass voice boomed out the Verdi aria.

One more singer later, a no-hoper with a rotten voice and

poor Italian, and then the screen was folded away and taken out by Janet and a policewoman between them. David was bending over the table, deep in conversation with the public prosecutor, Baretti, policemen and the translator.

They sprang apart and up from their chairs when Freda and I approached. David beamed while Judge Baretti strode towards me with hand and arm outstretched, shook mine and spoke something jovial in his language of which I understood almost nothing. Freda happily could and the two of them chatted while uniformed officers left the room.

She and I then followed, while David, the prosecutor and the translator stayed behind.

'See you later,' he called to us, 'just as soon as we've interviewed him.'

I hopped along, with Freda's left arm through my right one, holding me close to her side, and my other arm clutching the crutch. We were about to enter the packed sitting room, the Hinsley room, as two policemen were ordering Frank to get up from his chair and go with them. The room fell silent, all eyes upon the oboist.

We continued to just stand at the doorway to give the police and Frank space to move. He and one of the policemen arrived at the door, while the other stood back to let them through.

Just at that moment Frank's eyes met ours. His face turned puce and the veins stood out on his forehead. His eyes glared and he yelled 'You bitches!'

He lunged at us, his guard falling back slightly as he powered towards us, knocking us both across the corridor. Freda let out a scream. I was mute with fear. The three of us fell to the ground, with Frank spreadeagled over us. I could hear Freda's head hit the wall with a thump, cutting short a throttled scream from her.

Frank raised his hands and caught us both by the throat. He held my chin, fortunately, rather than my neck, but then lowered his grip. I could see his eyes bulging with hatred and white spittle on his lips. He roared 'I'll kill you bitches!'

My windpipe began to compress and I was numb with shock. Then his hands released my throat and Freda's as I heard her make a choking cough and then gasp.

Policemen were pulling Frank upright, controlling his raging body. One police hat went flying up into the air as his prisoner struggled and spluttered.

'Bitches!' was Frank's insult of choice. Quite a limited vocabulary for an educated man.

Soon more hands were employed in restraining him and he was frogmarched along the corridor towards the Hume room, while Freda and I were surrounded by people all sporting looks of utter concern and amazement.

We were helped up, and half carried into the Hinsley sitting room and both gently lowered onto a deep leather sofa. I heard words such as 'Bring some tea – hot and sweet', 'Doctor?', 'Frank?', 'Poor things', and, most welcome of all, 'Leave them a minute to recover, that was a terrible attack.'

I looked at Freda, whose face was red and wet with tears. She was shaking, and I looked at my own hands and saw that they were too. She then turned to me, and within moments we were locked together in a close hug, both sobbing and sighing. Then she pulled back her head, looked into my face and forced a wide smile, while sniffing a few times.

'Hey, Kiddo. That was something, yeah? Wow! Who'd a thought it, Frank? You OK now?'

I nodded, and sat back, wiping my face with the back of my hand. Suddenly a handful of tissues was pressed into it, and I saw Pippa's kindly face smiling wanly. Her expression lightened when she saw Freda and me deciding to be heroic and cheerful about it.

I looked around the room. It was crowded. Everybody must have been summonsed there while we were listening to the suspects in the Hinsley room.

After some time, during which Freda and I each downed a mug of sweet tea (infused with a quarter tumbler of brandy produced from the bar adjoining the Hume sitting room), David appeared at the door. The general murmuring stilled and all attention focused on him.

'Well, I'm to tell you that two of your orchestra will not be returning with you. Edward is being questioned in relation to a crime committed some years ago here in Italy, and Frank has been charged with the vanjacking and attempted theft of your instruments.'

A gasp rose from the assembly. Before anyone could say anything, he continued.

'He has given us some leads to the others involved. It seems he got in with a bad lot, a gang of criminals, while he was living in Naples. They had kept in touch, and when he found they were in the Rome area, he tipped them off about the van. He told us he was really after Jackson's violin, either to steal it, or just to get at him.'

That began to sink in, and the silence of amazement was slowly broken by the murmur of comments. David looked at Freda and me on the sofa.

'You were right about his voice. Frank was the man arguing with his colleagues in the wood and hoping to bully you into silence with his phoney Mafia symbols and warnings couched in song. Only a musician could have thought of that! He believed you two had actually recognised him when you were in the wood, or at least that you had, Julia. He was convinced you would have given him away but that he had frightened you off. Anyway, he's on his way to Rome now to be questioned.'

Then he turned back to the company,

'However, ladies and gentlemen, there will still be police present, and you will still be held here until further notice. It is probable that we have not yet caught the killer or killers of Jackson and Nelson, as Frank has a strong alibi for the time when we believe that Jackson was being killed.'

At that he looked towards Vaclav who nodded gravely.

'Yes, after the rehearsal, which Frank conducted until Teddy came, Frank and I went to the chapel to go over my tenor part until lunchtime.'

'Well,' said Teddy. 'That let's him off that particular hook. This is a ghastly business and we all want to do what we can to help. The sooner we go back home, the better. Can we leave this room now?'

'Yes,' David agreed. 'But not the grounds. Stay on site until we say you can leave. There are still a few hours before supper, so relax everybody. Janet says the pool is open if anyone would like to go for a swim.'

He turned to my companion on the sofa.

'Freda, will you be ready to go back into the woods in a little while? We'd like you to show us just where you were standing when you heard the voices and saw the two out of the three men there. Say twenty minutes?'

I thought that was too much to ask of someone who had

just been half-strangled, but she was made of more intrepid material than I.

'Sure,' she said, rising from the sofa. 'Just give me time to go get something on my feet, rather than these sandals.'

People stood back, admiration written over their faces, to let her pass and leave. David winked at me (winked? He had never done that before), and said softly: 'I won't ask you to come, with your foot. I suggest you have a lie down until supper. I'll see you later. And thanks for all your help.'

Unsure whether to be annoyed by his patronising attitude, or relieved and pleased by his consideration, I did haul myself up from the comfortable sofa. Liz, the television producer, handed me my crutch, and I limped out and up to my room.

I lay on the bed, staring at the ceiling far higher above me than in the average British home. I closed my eyes and breathed deeply, realising how tense my whole body had become. At least my elbow no longer hurt, nor the back of my head. Thank goodness it had not made contact with the wall, as had Freda's. I was thinking how strong she was, in body and in character, when I drifted off.

Surfacing to consciousness an hour or so later, I rolled off the bed and limped to the window. The terrace was again peopled by relaxing musicians and technicians, sipping drinks, reading or chatting. Others were drifing in from the pool, with towels over their shoulders and wet hair clinging to their scalps. I went into the Piazza's living area and made myself a strong coffee, using the Italian espresso maker on the gas hob. Even though it was early evening and it could keep me awake, I felt I needed a boost to my fragile system.

By the time I went outside hoping to catch the last golden, warm rays of the sun before supper, there were just a few others still there. Most had gone indoors to get ready for supper. As I sat and basked in the waning sunshine, the last few stragglers left, not before asking solicitously how I was feeling. I assured them of my being totally fine and stayed there until the chair began to feel uncomfortable and a slight cool breeze blew.

I was reluctant to go inside as there were still twenty minutes remaining before the meal would be served. I wondered where the police party had got to which had gone up to the woods with Freda and decided to saunter down to the end of the garden in the hope of seeing their return.

My ankle was feeling stronger and less painful than it had, so it was with a feeling that life was being gently restored to well-being that I made my way along the central path between low formal hedges. I looked left, up at the corner of the sienna-toned hotel atop the high sheer rockface, and right, to see lights sparkling on the surface of the lake. Little did I dream that this could have been the last sight I saw.

CHAPTER 24

AS I REACHED THE GARDEN'S END, beyond the cypresses and fountain, and further than the rock stairway and the entrance to the swimming pool, I peered over the waist-high stone parapet to see if I could detect any motion in the woods.

No sign of David, Freda and the police party. The iron gate to the pool was closed, but the narrower one leading to the rock stairway was open. All was quiet, with just birdsong from the woods and the chirrup of crickets. I wandered alongside the end wall from the cliff to the lake side and back again, looking out at the late summer foliage and the way the magnificent sunlight magnified some of the trees and the shade diminished others. Musing and humming quietly, I let myself be calmed and soothed by the tranquility of the spot.

Suddenly a sound intruded, to my irritation. I was no longer alone. From behind one of the cypresses someone was talking, quietly and in fluent Italian, into a mobile phone. I hoped it was not Fabio. I did not want to see him again, ever.

Somehow, with David's reappearance, my feelings towards both men had changed.

My heart began to beat faster as thoughts pounded in my head. Did my fling with Fabio weigh an even balance with David's affair? Was I as guilty as he in flouting my marriage vows, or was the marriage itself over in fact, if not in law? Did I still love David, despite everything? Would I sleep with Fabio again if circumstances warranted? Had I simply used Fabio in the way men use women, only to discard them as so much rubbish afterwards?

God, what was I thinking that I could stoop so low? David, I realised, was the only one, whatever he had done.

Just then the caller stepped from behind the tree and noticed me. Thank goodness, Robinson, not Fabio.

'Hi there Julia. How're you feeling now? Ghastly business.'

'Oh fine, thanks. I've rested. It's so lovely here, with the sun ...'

'Certainly is. Freda back yet? Very brave of her to go.'

'No, not yet. Thought I'd come out here to meet them.'

We both stood, leaning on the parapet, looking out at the trees, deep in thought.

I remembered when I first met Robinson, in Jackson's shadow. He was wearing a bright Hawaiian shirt, but his facial features were dull and grey. He broke into my thoughts, as something began nagging at me, causing a lump in my stomach, but I could not identify what was causing it.

'Frank, eh? What a bastard. Those instruments not only cost a fortune, but they mean a lot to us too.'

I murmured my agreement, but my unease was increasing. I do not know why I said it, but –

'You knew Frank from Naples, didn't you? Didn't I hear that you'd played with him, and Edward?'

'Only for a time. Vaclav was there too, more recently. But yes, I'd been in Italy a few years. No idea that Frank would turn out like that. And what was Edward's crime, did your husband tell you?'

Something made me not want to pursue this, nor to stay with Robinson. I wanted to go back, at once. I put my hand on my bag, ready to take it, but was impelled by some overwhelming need to know, to ask one question, unrelated to anything we were talking about.

'That shirt, that bright blue Hawaiian shirt. You wore that the day I first met you, and ...'

'What about it?' he tensed up suddenly and turned to face me. His eyes had narrowed. Now I was afraid.

'You wore it, didn't you, to that last rehearsal, on Friday? You were in the corridor when I just left my room after having got back from hospital. Nearly lunchtime, so after the rehearsal, you were walking in front of Nelson. He was carrying his doublebase case so I couldn't see past it properly, but I caught sight of your shirt, your bright blue Hawaiian one. Then you turned the corner ...'

The enormity of what I had just revealed was lost on neither of us. I turned to ice, and gulped, as Robinson glowered, his eyes taking on the chilling stare a big cat makes before pouncing on its prey. Then his hand shot out to my bag. Forced from my grip, with one sweeping motion, he threw it over the side of the parapet down into the woods. As I gasped my disbelief, my right hand found my crutch. I grabbed it tight and I swung it hard at Robinson, against whose body it made little impact. He simply reached out with his left hand, held it and prised it from my grip, flinging it behind him as if it were a matchstick. He then placed both his hands under my armpits and lifted me from the ground to sit me in the parapet.

'What the hell are you doing?' I cried, looking around desperately. We were hidden by the ornamental cypress trees from the sight of anyone who might have been outside or at a window.

'See your bag down there?'

I turned and looked down. I could indeed see my bag on the path below the wall, thirty or more feet below. I turned back. His eyes were flashing, catching the sun's rays, but with an intensity of emotion I would not have thought him capable of feeling. In measured tones, with a glacial menace, he explained,

'You leant over to see where it went and, oh dear, fell topsy-turvy over the wall. What a shame. Fatal, no doubt.'

'For God's sake, why? I won't tell anyone, honest, about the shirt.'

In times of crisis my grammar fails.

'Too right you won't.' He began to push me dangerously close to the outer edge of the parapet.

'Stop, please. Why? Did you kill Jackson? I thought you and he ...'

'You thought wrong. That bastard! He pushed me once too far. He wore me down with his bullying and his constant putting me down. Do you know what it's like, always being the butt of jokes, always being made to look stupid in front of people? It's shit, that's what. For years I let him get away with it. I didn't have the bottle to stop him. I owed him money and he could have called the debt in anytime. But then he mocked Alice, my daughter. He said he failed her because she was too much like me ... Like me, no talent, he said. Useless at the violin, and useless in life. Yes, I was useless, letting him ruin me. Marcia left me, because of that. Took Alice with her. I had nothing, nothing. But I could play the violin, yes I could. And I was a bloody good teacher. Ask Wing, ask anyone.'

I was glad of this speech; it gave me time to gather myself, to gain some strength to resist the next time he would push me. That could be the last time. I must stall him. I must keep him talking.

'Yes, I know you can,' I said, ingratiatingly. 'You're a brilliant violinist. I can see why Jackson had to go. He deserved it. But why Nelson?'

'Nelson?' He seemed slightly surprised, he relaxed his grip as he had to think for a moment.

'Oh yes, well Nelson hated Jackson too, just like Frank did. We all did. After the rehearsal, I went back to have it out with Jackson. Just before we went in, he had told me that he had failed Alice. Then he sniggered at me during the practice. When I came in late at one point he made a great show of how that had put him off, and we all had to go back and play it again. Then when I heard he was staying behind to practise his precious 'Devil's Trill' – the right piece for him, don't you think?'

I nodded vigorously. Anything to placate him right now. I saw that he was not really looking at me, but as if at something within himself, this dark place where murder was reasonable and just.

He picked up his story, talking in a sort of monotone, 'I decided to go back and stand up to him. I met him in the little area outside the conference room. He had gone for a piss. I told him what I thought of him, and he laughed in my face and turned to go back into the room. You can put someone down just so long. Nobody can take it for ever. I just picked up the nearest thing, that stone doorstop, and crashed it down over his head. It was a heavy bugger and killed him at once. A lot of blood, over me, over the floor.'

'How awful!' I commented, quickly adding, 'For you... How awful for you!'

But he did not hear, and just continued his recital, 'Nelson had been inside, packing up his base, when he heard us arguing. He saw everything. Didn't say anything, just helped me out. It was like he had wanted to do that to Jackson too. We lugged the body outside — bloody ton weight — and chucked it down one of those holes, cave things, in the rock, behind that stupid statue of someone. Then we cleaned up, using the towels and paper in the loo, throwing them, and the stone thingy, down the hole too.'

'But your shirt?'

'Yeah, covered in blood, as was Nelson's. We rushed to our rooms. That's when you must have seen us, on the corridor. We took the shirts off and wrapped them into a parcel and buried them somewhere out there.' He gestured with his head towards the woods.

'But Nelson?'

Robinson tightened the grip on my arms, his face contorted with the agony of remorse.

'Shut up! That's enough. I don't have to explain everything

to you. I didn't want to, of course not. Nelson was a good man, a friend. He had helped me out. But I just had to get rid of him. He told me early this morning, that he couldn't live with what he'd done, what we'd both done. He was about to go to that husband of yours and tell him everything.'

Just then he jolted me backwards with force, leaning over me. I managed to scream. Not as high and loud as I meant to, as my chest was constrained under his weight. I felt my bottom was over the edge, hanging in space, leaving just the back of my legs in contact with the ledge of the parapet. Thank God it was so deep. I thrust my heels against the wall to give me balance while his hands were forcing my shoulders back and down.

At one heart-stopping moment I felt myself teetering over, on the very point of falling. Then suddenly, just as I gasped with terror, the pressure of Robinson's hands was released. Someone pulled at and held tight to my legs and other hands were grabbing my hands and arms.

I could see Freda's furious face behind Robinson's, her arm around his throat, pulling him away from me. I was jerked upright and forwards off the wall, my face making contact with the buttons on the chest of a uniformed man. I was righted and stood there, in the most welcome company of police officers.

Freda shoved the deflated Robinson towards David who, with a uniformed officer, wrenched his hands behind his back and handcuffed them. The senior official, the prosecuting magistrate, put his hands on my shoulders to check that I could stand unaided, then Freda interposed, pulled me to herself and we hugged, rocking back and forth, until I slowly detached myself and we just smiled at each other. David stopped to pick up the crutch, handed it to me and took my other arm.

'OK to walk?' I nodded and together, police, prosecutor, Freda, David and I went, at my pace, along the path towards the Villa, with Robinson, squirming in an officer's grip, being pushed along ahead of us.

EPILOGUE

Three months later

WELL, HERE I AM, back in Gloucestershire. In London, Louisa was back with her boyfriend and pleased to have me out of the way. Ronald gave up the lease on his flat. My in-laws welcomed me once again into their home. Fortunately, it is spacious enough to accommodate all of us adequately. By 'us', I mean the two elderly Deanes and Maria, their new Filippina full-time carer, plus my own mother Helena and Ronald, as well as Melissa who had been their neighbour.

David, the pivot of the entire ménage, got on reasonably well with Maria, extremely well with Melissa and hardly at all with Helena and Ronald. I was once again immersed in this domestic scenario and acting as something of a bridge between those who were primarily my responsibilities and those who were his.

David went back to work with the Gloucestershire Police, and was delighted to receive an official commendation, in the form of a decorated certificate, from the Italian police for his help in solving the various crimes. His own superior had regarded it as a badge of honour for the County Police Service and hinted that David would be in line for promotion the next time the opportunity arrived.

The orchestra flew back home after Robinson's arrest and detention. We travelled in several small groups, according to domestic and work needs and seat availability on the flights. Teddy promised us all a reunion banquet in the new year, and many of us would meet again in Italy to attend and address various court hearings. Freda promised to stay with us whenever her schedule allowed and has already spent a weekend here. We laughed a lot and she sang some of Schubert's lieder to my in-laws, who were delighted.

Since our return I have been helping Liz put together her television series – rather different in outcome than that for which she had originally prepared. Yet the BBC was happy to take it, although cautious that nothing could be transmitted that could bring a charge of perverting the course of justice, or whatever law applies in Italy, with the criminal cases against Edward, Frank, and Robinson still to be heard. I could do most of the work on-line, although made a few trips to the capital to be filmed or have the voice-over recorded and re-recorded. Once was never enough.

My application was accepted for the post of temporary English teacher at the Cheltenham Ladies College to cover maternity leave for the spring term. After that, who knows?

David and I? Well, to mangle a quotation from Tobias Smollett's *The Expedition of Humphrey Clinker*:

'Let me be never so jarring and discordant, [David] puts

me *in tune*; and, like treble and bass in the same concert, [we] make excellent music together.'

According to my pregnancy tester, I could be needing some leave myself in seven months time ...

Made in the USA
Lexington, KY
27 May 2018